Life Can Be Murder

Rich Bishop Novels, Volume 6

Larry Darter

Published by Fedora Press, 2024.

LIFE CAN BE MURDER

First edition. April 9, 2024.

Copyright © 2024 Larry Darter.

ISBN: 979-8990455405

Written by Larry Darter.

For Molly, the best granddaughter ever.

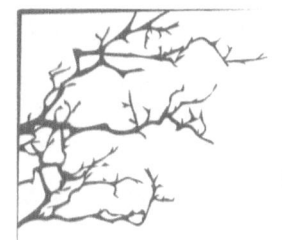

Chapter 1

THE PHONE RANG WHILE I was trying to decipher the clue, "Symbol of purity or spirituality" and guess the five letter word for thirty-four across on Monday's Honolulu Star-Advertiser crossword puzzle. I put down the stubby pencil and picked up the receiver.

"Bishop Detective Agency," I said into the phone.

"What?" said the female caller.

"Hi, Sally."

Sally Jayne Fisher was my gorgeous, wealthy Australian green-eyed blonde, with a figure to die for, girlfriend. And the love of my life.

"Well?" Sally asked.

"Well, what?"

"Well, what happened to the catchy slogan you always answer the phone with?"

"Bishop Detective Agency is enough. I've decided to conduct my business on a more professional level."

"Why?"

"I think it's time, don't you?"

"No, Rick. You will only confuse everyone and start all kinds of rumors."

"Rumors?"

"Common talk. People will start saying you're just another private investigator. Nothing special."

"I don't care. I'm tired of defending myself and needed a change."

"You haven't defended yourself since primary school, Rick."

"Are you forgetting last night on your living room sofa, Sally?"

"Rick!"

"Don't give me that sweet innocence stuff, darling. You should have rewarded me for that vigorous defense of my virtue."

"Didn't I?"

"Miss Fisher! Have you no shame?"

"Oh, Rick. Don't be a drongo, you root rat."

I glanced at the door as it swung open and a portly gentleman stuck his head in. "Mr. Bishop?"

"Something I can do for you?"

"Me?" Sally asked.

"No, hold on, Sally."

"Yes, if you're Richard Bishop," the man said.

"Client?" Sally asked.

"I think so, babe," I replied. "I haven't seen a subpoena yet."

"Awesome. Talk to you later, darling. Good luck."

"Bye," I said.

"Bye."

Sally hung up, and I replaced the receiver.

"Well, get it over with," I said to my visitor. "Hire me or serve me."

"I beg your pardon?"

"Forget it. Come in, and close the door quietly. I don't want you to wake my landlady."

"Your landlady?"

"Yes, she owns the Chinese herbal shop on the first floor. She's cranky enough without getting woke up early from her afternoon nap by slamming doors."

"Thank you," the man said, closing the door and crossing the room.

"Sit down, Mr..."

"O'Donnell. Laurence O'Donnell," he said, settling into the chair in front of my desk.

O'Donnell was prodigiously heavy with a reddish face, longish thick white hair, and heavy caterpillar brows to match. He wore a gray pin-striped, tailored three-piece suit with a gold watch chain stretched across his prosperous paunch.

"What can I do for you, Mr. O'Donnell?"

"I would like to hire you, if it's agreeable."

"For three-hundred a day plus expenses, I'm pretty agreeable."

"That's fine. I am prepared to pay you generously."

"How generously and for what?"

"Twenty-five hundred dollars for a quick trip to San Diego to pick up a package and return with it," O'Donnell said.

He withdrew a long, thick leather wallet from inside his jacket, and counted out twenty-five crisp one-hundred-dollar bills.

"You could get an average size package delivered from San Diego next business day by FedEx for a few hundred bucks. Or if it's something extremely valuable, Brinks could handle an insured shipment for you for less than a thousand. Why pay me twenty-five hundred to go get it for you?"

When people wanted to throw money at me, it always made me suspicious.

"I am quite capable of understanding the type of service I require, Mr. Bishop," O'Donnell said, dropping the impressive stack of hundreds on my desk.

"What's in the package? Cocaine or heroine? I'm not a drug mule."

"Nothing like that. It's an artifact. An ancient and rare Hawaiian artifact that is worth a fortune. I'm a dealer in antiquities and wish to repatriate the artifact for the benefit of the Bishop Museum. By chance, have you ever heard of a lei niho palaoa, Mr. Bishop?"

"Of course. I'm a native Hawaiian, Mr. O'Donnell. A lei niho palaoa is a Hawaiian necklace traditionally worn by ali'i. They commonly comprise a whale's tooth carved into a hook-shape pendant suspended by plaited human hair."

"Mr. Bishop, I'm pleased to learn you understand Hawaii's rich cultural history. This particular lei niho palaoa belonged to King Kalani'opu'u, uncle of Kamehameha. He gifted it to British navigator and cartographer Captain James Cook when he sailed into Kealakekua Bay in 1779."

"Antiquity smuggling is as illegal as narcotics smuggling, Mr. O'Donnell."

"Don't worry, Mr. Bishop. The customs papers are filed and everything is in order."

"Why can't you go and get it yourself?"

"The job will be quick and simple, but it is not without risks."

"What's risky about it?"

"Andrew Weismann, a rival antiquities dealer, will be awaiting the arrival of someone to pick up the artifact."

"And that's a problem?"

"Yes, he will try to stop you."

"How?"

"He will kill you if he believes it is necessary."

"That statement just cost you another twenty-five hundred," I said.

"I anticipated that," O'Donnell said, counting out another twenty-five crisp Benjamins. He placed the second stack on top of the first. "Five thousand then, and there will be another five thousand when you deliver the package safely to me here in Honolulu."

"Only if I live long enough to collect it. Why did you pick me for the job, Mr. O'Donnell?"

"I wanted to commission the best man available to retrieve the artifact from San Diego."

"Oh, you must have seen my Yelp reviews. I hope I can count on you for a five star review after I complete the job for you."

O'Donnell dismissed my remark and carried on with his instructions.

"You must leave for San Diego tomorrow. Go to the Hotel Del Coronado, where I will have a room reserved for you. On Wednesday afternoon, a Mr. Albert Brooks, an associate of mine, will meet you at the hotel to give you the artifact. I will email him your name and description and he will make the contact. Then you will return to Honolulu with the package on Thursday."

I agreed to meet him at my office early on Thursday afternoon after I returned with the item. He gave me a printed confirmation for a round-trip ticket on American Airlines, a sweaty handshake, and a smile that reminded me of a man who had swallowed a mouthful of sour milk.

In my business, I expect trouble and can usually spot it faster than a lonely hot blonde. And as I watched the door close behind Laurence O'Donnell, I spotted trouble all over the place and I figured Rick Bishop was about to be up to his shoulder holster in it.

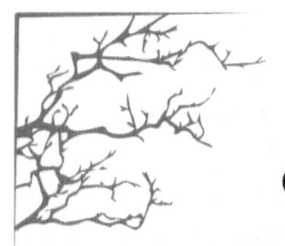

Chapter 2

SINCE I HAD TAKEN IN more money in a single day than I usually earned during a good month, I thought a celebratory drink was in order. Sliding open the bottom drawer of my desk, I pulled out the fifth of Old Rip Van Winkle bourbon, but found the bottle was empty. I pressed it down on top of the trash in my overflowing waste basket and stood up.

Picking up the pile of cash, I slipped two thousand into my wallet and carried the rest over to my office safe. After dialing the combination and opening the safe, I took out the envelope that I had marked with "Rainy Day Fund" and added the remaining three thousand to the thirty-seven cents already inside the envelope. Then I slotted it back inside the safe, closed the door, and spun the dial.

Glancing at the wall clock, I saw it was nearly one in the afternoon. Close enough, I thought. I slaved away from eleven in the morning until two in the afternoon four days a week and figured I deserved to knock off a little early for once. After all, all work and no play made Rick a dull boy. I'd grab a nice lunch down at the Ala Moana Center food court, drop by the liquor store to resupply my office liquor cabinet, and head over to the Likelike, the dive bar owned by my best friend, Joe Rose, to kill time before dinner at Sally's condo.

I locked up the office and took the stairs down to the street entrance singing "We're In the Money," as I descended. "We're in the money, we're in the money; we've got a lot of what it takes to get along!" After pushing out through the glass door and locking it, I turned to walk to my car and almost ran into my curmudgeonly old landlady, Mrs. Wong, who was sweeping the sidewalk with her ridiculous short-handled fan broom. She stood erect, and brushed a strand of gray hair out of her eyes that had escaped the severe bun at the crown of her head, and scowled at me.

"Mr. Rick," she said, pointing a bony finger in my face accusingly. "Your rent ten days past due. You pay now or I evict you again. You hear, Mr. Rick?"

"Mrs. Wong," I said, flashing her my best smile. "What a pleasant surprise running into you. Yes, I'm sorry about the rent. I've just been swamped with work and it slipped my mind."

I reached for my wallet and carefully picked nine one hundred-dollar bills out of it and offered them to Mrs. Wong with a flourish.

"There you are, Mrs. Wong. I added an extra hundred for the inconvenience. Buy yourself something real nice. Maybe get a new broom down at Aloha Dollar. Using that thing you've got there must be murder on your back with all the stooping over."

Mrs. Wong snatched the bills and then held each one up individually to the sunlight to gauge their authenticity. Satisfied I hadn't stuck her with counterfeits, she shoved the money into the pocket of her floral house dress and returned to her sweeping without a word.

I strolled to my car at the curb and clicked the key fob. Just as I opened the door of my Ford Mustang convertible, Mrs. Wong shouted at me.

"Yes, Mrs. Wong," I said, turning back to her.

"I tell you, parking reserved for customer, Mr. Rick. You park in back. You hear, Mr. Rick?"

"Yes, Mrs. Wong. Have a nice day."

I got in the Mustang, cranked the engine, and merged into the Hotel Street traffic.

IT WAS GOING ON THREE in the afternoon when I parked the Mustang in the lot at the Likelike Club. My friend Joe and I had served together in the SEAL teams until we had both tired of the thankless job of spreading democracy in far-flung countries across the globe where the people had a zero interest in democracy and weren't even sure what it was.

Joe, always the thrifty sort, had saved a bundle during our years in the Navy. As soon as we got out, Joe bought a rundown dive bar off Waikiki steps from the beach and he renamed it the Likelike. With a lot of sweat equity, he completely remodeled the place and transformed the club into the most stylish dive bar in Honolulu.

I spent a lot of my recreational time at the Likelike because, of course, I wanted to support my best friend's business. But I admit it helped that Joe practically forced free drinks on me whenever I visited his establishment.

Joe was sitting at his usual corner of the bar reading the paper when I walked in and Eddie Ka'ahea was tending the bar.

"Hey, cousin," Eddie said. "The usual?"

"Yes, thanks, Eddie," I said, climbing on the stool next to Joe.

Eddie pulled a bottle of Longboard Island Lager out of the cooler behind the bar, but just as he was about to pop the top, Joe snapped his fingers and pointed at him.

"Don't serve him until you see his money," Joe said.

Eddie paused and gave me an apologetic look.

"What's your problem, Joe?" I asked. "I always pay."

"You never pay, Richard," Joe replied. "Your tab is up to five hundred bucks again. I'm cutting off your credit, pal."

"You wound me, Joe," I said, reaching for my wallet.

Taking five crisp Benjamins out of it, I slapped them on the bar next to Joe.

"I'd never want it said I don't pay my obligations in a timely manner."

Joe gaped at me in astonishment and then scooped up the bills and handed them to Eddie.

"Okay, he can have the beer now," Joe said to Eddie before glancing back at me.

"I hate to break it to you, Richard, but people have been calling you a freeloader since the day I met you. What gives? Where did you get the dough?"

"Joe, you're not the only successful entrepreneur in Honolulu. I do okay in the private investigations business."

Joe hooted with laughter and jerked a thumb at me as he looked back at Eddie.

"Get a load of Sam Spade here, will you? He's a successful businessman now."

Eddie flashed a toothy grin and set the bottle of Longboard on the bar in front of me.

"What kept you, Richard?" Joe asked. "You're usually here at two-fifteen on the dot."

"Well, I treated myself to a leisurely lunch after work before coming here."

"You get your usual, the Big Mac meal at Mickey D's on your way over?"

"Joe, I don't eat every meal at McDonalds, you know."

"Since when?"

"I lunched at the Ala Moana Center food court. Thank you very much."

"Wow, last of the big spenders," Joe chuckled. "You really must be rolling in the dough. Get another divorce case?"

"No, I've got an important case on the mainland. I'm flying out tomorrow morning."

"Where to?"

"San Diego. I'm staying at the Hotel Del Coronado."

"Coronado?"

"Yes, that's right," I said, sipping my beer.

Joe and I first met when we were both going through the twenty-four week BUD/S course, the Navy SEALs Basic Underwater Demolition/SEAL "A" school at the Naval Special Warfare Training Center in Coronado.

"We're in the presence of greatness, Eddie," Joe said. "The man and the legend. Richard Bishop, the globetrotting gumshoe."

"Go ahead and laugh, Joe. But the Bishop Detective Agency is a growing concern."

I spent the afternoon at the Likelike drinking beer and reminiscing with Joe about our days in BUD/S. He was in a better mood than usual since I'd paid my bar tab in full. At six-thirty, I left the bar for Sally's condo on Kapiolani Boulevard.

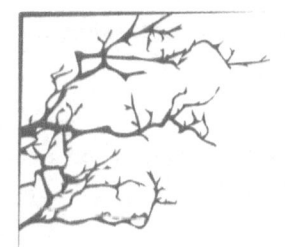

Chapter 3

AFTER I RANG THE DOORBELL, Cooper, Sally's houseman, opened the door.

"Good evening, Mr. Bishop."

"Evening, Cooper. You look like you're going out."

"Yes, sir. Miss Fisher wants me to go down to the butcher for some steaks to grill for dinner."

"Ah, where is Miss Fisher?"

"In the lounge, sir."

"Okay, see you later, Cooper."

I went in and walked into the living room, or lounge, as the Aussies called it.

"Ally, ally, oxen free," I said cheerfully to Sally.

"Ricky, hi," she said, hugging me and giving me a peck on the lips.

"Hi," I said, when she pulled away. "Well, check out that outfit."

Sally had on a pair of scandalously short and tight spandex shorts and a color coordinated sports bra.

"Is that what the modern woman wears when lounging around the house this season?"

"No, silly. I just finished my yoga workout."

"I guess we're staying in tonight?"

"Uh-huh. I just sent Cooper out to get some steaks for the barbie."

"I met him at the door."

"I'll just go and chuck on some tracky dacks and then I've got a few things to do in the kitchen. Why don't you relax on the sofa and take it easy until dinner is ready?"

"Okay, but I'm a little tired. I might fall asleep."

"Hear, read this if you want to stay awake," Sally said, sweeping a magazine off the coffee table and offering it to me.

"Oh, swell," I said, looking at the magazine. "True Detective. Who sends you these things? The corpse of the month club?"

Sally smirked. "I won't be long."

Yawning, I sat down on the sofa, flipped open the magazine, and tried to read the first story.

"It was going on midnight and fog encircled the old house like a thin wet blanket. The silhouette of a man crept stealthily across the graveled garden path..."

The next thing I knew, Sally woke me for dinner. We sat down at the dining room table and Cooper served up the steaks, baked potatoes, and a garden salad.

"So, did your visitor hire you for a case?" Sally asked.

"Yes, yes he did," I said. "And I collected a fat retainer."

"Good on ya," Sally said. "What sort of case is it, darling?"

"I have to go to the mainland to retrieve a valuable artifact," I said. "I'm flying out tomorrow morning and will be gone until Thursday."

"Where are you going?"

"San Diego."

"Oh, isn't that where you and Joe met?"

"That's right. I'm staying at a hotel near to the base where we did our military training together."

"You know, I could take a few days off work and go with you," Sally said. "I've never been to San Diego."

"Oh, I wish I could take you along, babe. But not this trip. My client warned me it could be dangerous."

"Ricky, I so wish you wouldn't accept the dangerous assignments."

"It comes with the territory, and don't worry, honey. I'm a big boy and can take care of myself."

"Doesn't going into harm's way frighten you?"

"Not really. You get used to it."

"Perhaps after dinner, when we retire to the bedroom, I'll give you a proper fright by making you defend your virtue again," Sally smirked.

"Oh, dear," I said. "I better practice my knee knocking first, so I won't disappoint you."

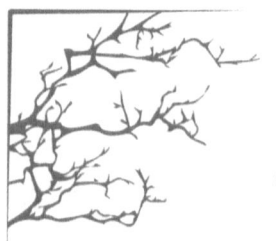

Chapter 4

COOPER DROPPED ME AT the departure terminal at Honolulu's Daniel K. Inouye International Airport on a clear, sunny Tuesday morning and an hour later I boarded an 11 a.m. flight for San Diego. Having flown so often while in the military, I found the flight about as interesting as a bus ride.

About five hours after departing Honolulu, the plane passed over the Southern California coastline north of downtown. After continuing inland for several miles, the plane banked right in a sweeping lazy turn to line up with the runway.

Having flown into San Diego many times before, looking out my window on the left side of the aircraft after the turn, I saw the familiar urban sprawl. The plane continued to descend as we passed over Balboa Park. After a quick glimpse of the San Diego–Coronado Bridge, the skyscrapers of downtown appeared seemingly just outside my window for the last minute or so before the plane touched down on the runway.

After deplaning, I caught a shuttle in front of the terminal for the rental car center, rented a Toyota Corolla, and took the 5 south to Coronado Island. I arrived at the Hotel Del Coronado and turned the rental over to a valet at 8:30 p.m. local time. After checking in I dropped my roll-aboard carry on, my only luggage, off at my room and went back down to have dinner.

After settling on The Laundry Pub, an eatery offering classic pub fare and local craft beer located inside the hotel's beautifully restored laundry building, I had a burger and fries and a few craft beers. The pub, decorated in the style of an 1880s-era bar, featured original brickwork, vaulted ceilings, and the laundry's early conveyor system above restored hardwood floors.

After dinner, I went back up to my room. I called Sally, and told her I would ship her back some oranges. After we hung up, I showered, brushed my teeth, and called it a night.

O'DONNELL HADN'T GIVEN me a time when my contact was supposed to arrive. He had only said his associate, Albert Brooks, would meet me at the hotel sometime on Wednesday afternoon. I rolled out of bed at 10 a.m. and had a beachside breakfast at the Del's beachfront food truck and bar trailer. Then I collected the rental from the valet and toured the sights of Coronado Island to kill some time.

At 2:00 p.m., I returned to the hotel, went up to my room, and took a shower to lose some of the stiffness from sitting in the car all day. I'd already had lunch in town, so I went downstairs to the Babcock & Story Bar to see if I could get some of the stiffness back. It was a little more glamorous than The Laundry Pub I'd tried the previous evening and boasted live music. I sat at the large mahogany bar sipping Blue Moon beer.

About an hour after I sat down, an attractive blonde walked up beside me.

"Is this seat taken?" she asked.

"Nope, have a seat," I replied.

"Thank you," she said, sitting on the stool next to mine. "It's nice and cool in here."

"Yeah, can I get you something to go with the air conditioning?"

"Thank you. A Hemingway's daiquiri."

I didn't know what it was, but it didn't matter since she was drinking it. So I flagged the bartender.

"A Hemingway's daiquiri for the lady and another Blue Moon." Then I looked over at the blonde. "Are you staying at the hotel?" I asked.

"Yes. Are you?"

"Just got in last evening."

"My name is Martin. Marlee Martin."

"Richard Bishop."

"Hello, Richard Bishop."

"Staying in San Diego long?"

"Depends on the weather."

The bartender set her cocktail on the bar, along with another beer for me.

"Cheers," she said, lifting her drink.

"To the weather," I said, touching my bottle to her glass. "What kind of weather are we drinking to, anyway?"

"Sun, rain. Any kind of weather as long as there is something to do."

"Then let's drink to something to do," I said.

She smiled and sipped her drink, and I drank some beer.

"What do you do, Mr. Bishop?"

"I start by asking attractive blondes to call me Rick."

She smiled again. "All right, Rick. What do you do?"

"Make a few bucks. Work when I have to. Enjoy a cool drink in a bar with a woman named Marlee sometimes."

"Are you married, Rick?"

"Not a bit," I said, holding up my ring-less left hand. "Never made the trip. How about you?"

"Once. I didn't like the weather. Why don't you buy me dinner this evening, Rick?"

"I'm sorry you said that."

"Oh? You already have a date?"

"Business. Then I have to fly right back to Honolulu."

"Well, it was a nice idea," Marlee said.

"The nicest," I said, standing up and leaving cash on the bar to cover the tab. "Well, I've got to be going."

"Nice meeting you, Rick."

"Likewise. Goodbye, Marlee."

"Bye, Rick."

As I turned to walk away, she spoke again.

"Rick."

"Yes?"

"What's the weather like in Honolulu?"

"Warm and sunny when I left," I said. Taking out a pen, I wrote my phone number on a cocktail napkin and left it on the bar. "If you ever fly out, call me."

"I'll do that. Maybe we can find a secluded beach and work on getting rid of our tan lines."

"That sounds like a lovely idea," I said with a grin.

I left Marlee sitting at the bar looking lonely and went back up to my room to lie down to rest, feeling a little light-headed and weak in the knees.

I must have dozed off because when I woke up and looked at my watch it was nearly eight. My contact was overdue, so I sat up and thought about what I should do about it.

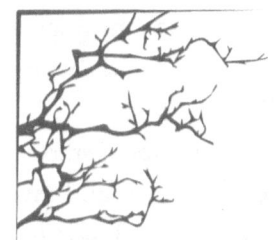

Chapter 5

AT EIGHT-THIRTY, I called the front desk. When the clerk answered, I identified myself and asked if anyone had called or come in looking for me.

"No, sir. There are no messages."

"You're sure?"

"Yes, sir."

"Okay, thanks."

Hanging up the phone, I considered calling O'Donnell back in Honolulu. Surely he had some way of reaching his associate. But just as I dialed the number, someone knocked on my door.

"It's about time," I grumbled, getting off the bed.

I hung up, crossed the room, and opened the door. A man pushed by me and staggered into the room.

"Close the door," he groaned.

"Hey, what's the idea?" I demanded.

"Close it."

Closing the door, I turned to glare at my rude guest.

"Look, pal, you better..."

He interrupted. "Listen. Go to... Mission Bay..."

"Hey, you're hurt," I said, realizing the guy was pale and barely coherent.

"Mission Bay..." he groaned, before falling to the floor.

"Hey," I shouted. I knelt beside him and pressed my fingers to his throat, checking for a pulse. "Oh swell," I said. "Why does everyone have to pick my room to die in?"

He was lying on his back with his eyes still open, staring at the ceiling, but seeing nothing. I rolled him over and saw a hole in his suit jacket. When I lifted the jacket, I saw his blood-soaked light blue shirt had a matching hole and wondered how far he had traveled with a bullet in his back.

The man was heavyset, with gray hair, and wearing an expensive suit. The identification in his wallet showed he was my contact, Albert Brooks. I searched him for the package even though I doubted he was concealing the Hawaiian artifact he was supposed to deliver. I sat down on the edge of the bed to think. He had said something about Mission Bay before he had died. Had he been trying to tell me where to find the artifact? That made little sense. I was familiar with Mission Bay, a San Diego neighborhood centered on its namesake waterway. It was a resort area known for Sea World, which had rides, aquariums, and aquatic animal shows. There was a huge man-made water sports zone, popular for sailing and kite surfing, on the western bay. It was such a large area, looking for the artifact there would be like looking for a needle in a million haystacks. I thought about the bonus I was going to be out of if I didn't bring the artifact back to O'Donnell and groaned.

Not wishing to sleep with a dead body in my room, I picked up the phone and called the front desk. I told them I had a stiff in my room and that they might want to notify the cops.

The first of Coronado's finest to arrive were two uniformed officers. Coronado wasn't only an island, but a resort city with its own police force. They came in, frisked me, and told me not to touch anything. One cop took my identification, and they watched me closely until the homicide people came.

They came in large numbers, as they always do. Crime scene technicians, a photographer, someone from the medical examiner's office, and two detectives to investigate the crime and me, the suspect. In this case, a detective named Lee Richardson from the homicide squad led the crew. I'm six foot one and he was taller than I was. Taller and thicker. His dark hair was closely cropped, and he was clean-shaven. His suit was immaculately pressed and his tie neatly knotted. He inspected my Hawaii driver's license and private investigator license the patrol cops had given him.

"Richard Bishop," he said thoughtfully, glancing at me.

"Six one, one hundred and ninety—licensed by the state of Hawaii—brown hair and the loveliest blue eyes," I said.

"I can read," Richardson snapped.

"But the printed description doesn't do me justice."

"You're a wise guy, aren't you?"

"The California propaganda must have influenced me."

"Well, you're a little out of your territory, Bishop. Your license carries no weight here in California."

"Maybe if I ate a big dinner."

"And I think you should know something. I don't like private detectives."

"What a coincidence," I said. "I don't care much for rude police detectives."

"How did you know him?" Richardson said, jerking his head towards the corpse on the floor.

"I never saw him before."

"You weren't expecting him?"

"No."

"You called the desk earlier and asked if anyone was looking for you."

"I always do that. I get lonesome staying in hotels."

"What are you doing in Coronado?"

"Industrial espionage. A Florida orange grower hired me."

"You know something, Bishop?"

"I know a lot of stuff."

"I feel like hauling you in for questioning."

"Better re-think it. I can get nasty."

"You're in trouble enough to pull up over your head and tie a bow in it."

"Call Lieutenant Chang, the homicide squad commander in Honolulu. He will vouch for me."

"I'll do that. But I still want to know why this guy picked your room to die in."

"All right," I said. "All right, I'll tell you. I flew here all the way from Honolulu just to confuse you."

"Yeah?"

"Yeah. I haven't killed a man in a hotel room with my imaginary gun for years. And I'm the compulsive type. I just couldn't help it."

"I think I'll arrest you and lock you up."

"Well, you could do that. But I would be out in an hour, and I'll sue your city for false arrest for so much you will be pounding a beat down in San Ysidro arresting drunk sailors on their way back from Tijuana."

"Look, Bishop, there's been a murder."

"Well, I didn't do it."

"The victim died in your room. You will have to stick around for questioning."

"Then question me."

"There's plenty of time. You look like the type who breeds trouble."

"Yeah, I took it up after I lost my pineapple plantation."

"I will not arrest you right now. But I think you're mixed up in this killing, and I'll find about it soon enough."

"Let me know when you do."

"You will be the first to hear about it."

I watched while the coroner's clean up boys hauled away my dead contact on a gurney, then I promised Detective Richardson I would meet at the Coronado Homicide Division at ten o'clock the next morning.

"And, Bishop..."

"Yeah, I know. Don't leave town."

They left my room, and I waited until I was sure they had cleared the hotel. Then I started thinking about Brooks' last words before he died. I doubted he would have told me to go to a neighborhood of over three square miles and probably close to fifty thousand people to find the artifact. But I figured there must be a lot of businesses there with Mission Bay as a prominent part of their business name. I pulled out my phone and did a quick internet search. The search yielded seven possibilities. Mission Bay Appliances, Mission Bay Brewing Company, Mission Bay Graphics, Mission Bay Paving Company, Mission Bay Moving & Storage, Mission Bay Bolt & Nut, and Mission Bay Baja Restaurant.

Out in front of the hotel, I found the valet absent from his stand. I started for the underground parking garage to look for him, but I never made it. I felt something hard pressed against my back.

"Hold it right there," a male voice growled.

"Give me one good reason," I said.

"This gun in your back."

"I'm glad you said that. For a moment, I was afraid you were just glad to see me."

"Don't try anything stupid. Who would know you tried being brave if you're dead?"

"What do I have to do to stay alive?" I asked.

"Be good and get into that gray car right there in front of you."

"Okay. Where are we going?" I asked, walking toward the car.

"What difference does it make?"

I reached for the door handle and opened the front passenger door. "Well, I might like to look at the scenery on the way."

"Sorry to disappoint you."

Suddenly, I felt a flash of pain behind my right ear and the world went black.

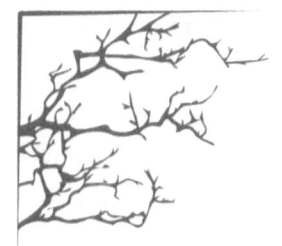

Chapter 6

HE HAD SAPPED ME BEHIND the ear with the gun barrel and I'd gone down like a cement block in a water well. I didn't know how long I had been unconscious, but when I came out of it and shook the cotton out of my head, someone was slapping my face lightly. I was inside a large metal building with a concrete floor and an enormous overhead door at one end, sitting in a chair looking at the biggest stomach I'd ever seen. My eyes traveled upward over the belly and a large, round red face appeared. It smiled, and I tried to return the courtesy, but my head hurt too much.

"Feeling better, Mr. Bishop?" the owner of the face asked.

"Well, I've felt better."

"Bryan."

"Yes, Mr. Weismann?"

"Get Mr. Bishop something to drink."

"Right away, Mr. Weismann."

I listened to footsteps on the concrete floor fading away.

"Let me find my head first," I said. "I wouldn't know where to pour it."

I found my wrists and forearms tied to the armrests of the chair and my ankles bound to the front chair legs.

"I rarely resort to violence," Weismann said.

"But this time, you made an exception?"

"I found it necessary. I wouldn't want you to find this place again."

As my vision cleared, I noticed an open door on one side about halfway to the overhead door at the end. I smelled the potent scent of oranges and figured the place must be close to a grove.

"I wouldn't want to after the trouble I had getting her the first time. What happens when I leave?"

I heard the footsteps returning across the concrete floor.

"That depends on how much you care to tell me while you're here."

"Here's your drink," the man called Bryan said.

He twisted the top off a bottle of water and put it to my lips and tipped it up. I swallowed as much as I could because my mouth felt like it was full of cotton, but most of the water dribbled down my chin onto my shirt and jacket.

"Thanks, pal," I said. "What happened to your big gun?"

"Would you like to see it?"

"Not especially."

"Enough levity," Weismann said. "Let's get down to business, Mr. Bishop. Shall we?"

"Levity," I said. "Humor or frivolity, especially the treatment of a serious matter with humor or in a manner lacking due respect."

"It seems Mr. Bishop is an educated man, Bryan. He reads classic literature."

"What kind of business did you want to discuss, Mr. Weismann?"

"You know who I am?"

"Yeah. Bryan here gave away your name and someone warned me about you."

"Then we understand each other. Where is it?"

"Where is what?"

"Come now, Mr. Bishop. I thought we had dispensed with the frivolous? The lei niho palaoa, of course."

"Have you tried museums?"

"Do you intend to persist with the humor, Mr. Bishop?"

"Only if it gets a laugh."

"Mr. Bishop, I intend to have the lei niho palaoa. We both know the artifact I refer to and that Mr. Brooks came to your hotel room this evening."

"Yeah, but all he brought along with him was a bullet in his back."

"We caught up with him when he landed, but he eluded us."

"And Bryan tried to slow him down with his big gun."

"Let's just say he met an unfortunate accident. Somewhere between the accident and your hotel room, he hid the lei niho palaoa. Where, Mr. Bishop?"

"He didn't mention it. Of course, he dropped dead as soon as he staggered into my room."

"Let's be reasonable, Mr. Bishop. I know Laurence O'Donnell promised you a five thousand dollar bonus if you deliver the artifact to him in Honolulu. I'll give you the five thousand to tell me where it is. You get your money and I get the lei niho palaoa."

"I can't do that. If word got out that I took bribes to betray my clients, I wouldn't be in business long. And I just invested a lot of money in getting my website redesigned. Besides, I still don't know what you're talking about."

Weismann sighed impatiently. "Come, come, Mr. Bishop. Bryan followed you all the way from Honolulu."

"Good for Bryan. He should get his tracking merit badge and that promotion from Tenderfoot."

"Look you..."

"Quiet, Bryan. I'm attempting to reason with Mr. Bishop. There is plenty of time for you to use your talents if he remains intractable. You can take the five thousand from me, Mr. Bishop. And you should."

"For five thousand, I'd sell you my grandmother's dentures, but I don't know what you're talking about."

"Very well," Weismann said. "Bryan, let's have some music."

"Yes, Mr. Weismann."

"I really don't feel much like dancing," I said. "I'm still a little dizzy."

The music blared. It sounded like ranchera, the regional Mexican music played by mariachi bands.

"Last chance, Mr. Bishop," Weismann said over the music.

"I'm still at a loss," I replied.

"Indeed, you are," Weismann said. "Bryan!"

"Is Bryan going to get rough?" I asked.

"Where is the artifact?"

"Sorry," I said. "Can't hear you for the music."

"Change his mind, Bryan."

"Certainly."

Bryan had donned a pair of black leather gloves. I only hoped they weren't the type with lead weights across the knuckles.

"Now look, I..."

The first blow was just an open hand slap across the face, but it was enough to make my eyes water.

"Where is it?" Weismann demanded.

"I tell you, I don't...."

The second blow was a left hook into my ribs that knocked the breath out of me.

"I don't know," I gasped.

Bryan gave me a right cross to the jaw that rattled my teeth and I tasted the blood in my mouth.

"Where is it, funny man?" Bryan growled.

"You can go straight to..."

Another punch in the ribs, this time on the right side that sent a spiderweb of pain along my entire right side.

"Where?" Weismann shouted.

"No," I said.

Bryan hit me again and again, alternating body blows with punches to the face, whip lashing my head to the side. I lost track of how many times he had hit me. Blood rushed down from my nose and across my lips. My vision darkened, a black fringe that fell down like the dropping of a theater curtain. If they hadn't tied me to the chair, I would have long since fallen off it onto the floor.

"Really, Mr. Bishop, is it worth all this?" Weismann said.

"No, but I wish you thought so," I wheezed before spitting out a mouthful of bloody saliva.

"All right, Bryan, continue."

Bryan punched me a few more times.

"This isn't necessary," I said between pants for breath.

"Just tell me where it is," Weismann said.

"I don't know."

"Maybe he's telling the truth," Bryan said, flexing the fingers of both hands. "Maybe Brooks didn't have the chance to tell him where he put it."

I figured his hands were swelling, but had no illusions punching me was hurting them more than he was hurting me. The black curtain was a little less pervasive than before, but threatened to drop again.

"Then he is of no use to us," Weismann said. "Then again, maybe Brooks told him. Mr. Bishop?"

"Huh?"

"He is an obstinate young man," Weismann said.

"I'll change that," Bryan said, pulling his gloves tighter, before going back to work.

"No, you will kill him. If he knows, he can still lead us to it. Put him to sleep and drop him off in an alley somewhere."

Bryan clocked me with a right-left combination, using his hips rather than his torso to generate the power behind the blows. The black curtain fell on the last act. After a brief burst of fireworks, everything dropped out from under me. I felt myself sailing through the darkness, wishing I was someone else. Finally, I slowed and started to fall into a black abyss. Just a poor, tired, beaten-up little private detective looking for a place to lay my head and rest.

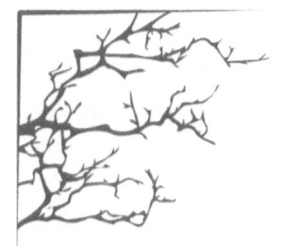

Chapter 7

WHEN I REGAINED CONSCIOUSNESS, I found myself sitting in an alley with my back against a trash dumpster. I thought of all my aches and pains and the money Weismann had offered me. I grabbed the lip of the dumpster and pulled myself to my feet and thought the bonus O'Donnell had offered me wasn't a penny more than I could have taken from Weismann and avoided getting beaten half to death. Or was it getting beaten seventy-five percent to death? Then I staggered out to the street, looking for a psychiatric ward where I could turn myself in for being an idiot. I spotted a cab before stepping out in front of it and getting run down and hailed it.

The brakes squealed, and the tires screeched as the cab stuttered to a stop. Leaning on the fender, I shouted to the driver.

"Hey, buddy, take me..."

"Rick!"

"What? Oh. Good evening, Miss Martin. You don't happen to have a spare unit of O positive on you, do you?"

"What in the world happened?"

"I went for a jog in an orange grove and got jumped by a mechanical citrus harvester."

Marlee put an arm around me to keep me upright.

"Here, let me help you in the taxi."

"I think you'll have to."

"I was just on my way back to the hotel. Go ahead driver."

Glancing back at me, she said, "I had the driver pull over when I saw you standing in the street."

"How convenient for me."

"What in heaven's name happened to you?"

"I was just jogging. Honest I was. Then that harvesting machine came at me out of nowhere."

"If you don't want to tell me."

"Let's take the swelling out of my head first."

"Do you want to go to the emergency room?"

"No, that's unnecessary. The hotel will be fine."

"I'll get you right up to your room."

"No, let's go to your room. I don't want to explain this to Richardson."

"Richardson? Who is that?"

"A very narrow-minded police detective I had the misfortune of meeting earlier this evening. He would never buy the citrus harvester story."

"Just lay your head on my shoulder, Rick."

"Which one?"

"This one, silly."

"No, I mean, which head?"

HOW I GOT THERE WAS a little foggy, but eventually I found myself on the bed in Marlee Martin's hotel room.

"I had the driver stop at a pharmacy on the way and got a first aid kit," she said, opening a little white box with a red cross on it.

Marlee ripped open a package of alcohol wipes.

"This will sting a little," she said.

"Use it on the numb spots."

Marlee wiped the cuts above my eyes.

"Ouch!"

"I'm so sorry. With the dried blood wiped away, I think it looked worse than it is and maybe you aren't hurt as bad as I first thought."

"Would you be more satisfied with, shall we say, a corpse?"

Marlee chuckled. "You will be all right, Rick."

She applied butterfly bandages to my cuts.

"Yeah, but I'm going to need a lot of nursing to pull through."

"Well, I would be happy to take care of that for you."

"In that case, I think I might survive after all."

"Are you going to tell me what happened?"

"I can't."

"Is it some sort of secret?"

"Yes. I don't want you getting involved in it."

"Hm. Just what kind of work do you do, Rick?"

"Whatever it is, I'm woefully underpaid."

"You must make some dangerous enemies."

"I try my best."

"I thought you were going back to Honolulu tonight?"

"I almost did, it a pine box. Hey..."

"What's the matter?"

"What time is it?"

"Almost four o'clock. It's morning."

"I need to sleep for a few hours and then I have to go to Mission Bay."

"Mission Bay? In Honolulu?"

"No, here in San Diego."

"What for?"

"I've got to find something there."

"Find what?"

"I can't say. It's business."

"Can I go with you?"

"No, you better stay here with the first aid kit. I might need more nursing when I get back."

I WOKE UP WITH SUNLIGHT lancing through the blinds. Glancing at the alarm clock on the nightstand, I saw it was after 10:30 a.m. and I had missed my appointment with Detective Richardson. But I couldn't worry about it now.

Looking over, I saw Marlee curled up on the other side of the bed. Thankfully, she was fully clothed except for shoes and so was I. Trying to convince Sally I had spent the night with a naked woman in her hotel room and nothing had happened would have been a bridge too far. And since Marlee wasn't naked, I saw no reason I would need to mention the spending the night in her room part.

Easing out of bed so I didn't wake her, I grabbed my shoes and carried them with me to the door. I opened it, went out, and eased the door closed behind me. Then I limped to the elevator, headed for my room. My entire body hurt, but at least I didn't feel faint.

After showering, I used a lint and hair removal brush I found in the closet to clean my suit as best I could. The brush did nothing for the wrinkles. After putting on a clean shirt, I put the suit back on and tied my shoes. Then I grabbed the memo book I'd written the names of the Mission Bay business names in and headed downstairs. The valet brought the rental car around and as I opened the door to get behind the wheel, a large arm shoved its way in front of me. Detective Richardson was on the other end of it.

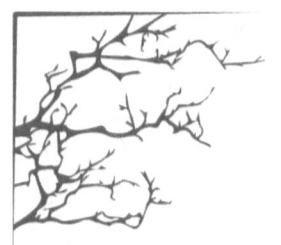

Chapter 8

RICHARDSON LOOKED ME up and down.

"Well, looks like you've been busy, Bishop."

"I'm sure you know the old saying about the dangers of idle hands, Detective."

"Where are you off to now?"

"To blow up city hall. Want to come along and hold the bomb for me?"

"Look, Bishop, I'm keeping score if the thought hasn't occurred to you."

"What do you do when the number goes past ten?"

"The only reason you're not in jail is because I called your friend Lieutenant Chang in Honolulu?"

"Yeah? What did David have to say about me?"

"He said he used to work with you when you were a homicide cop before you went over to the dark side. He said you stay on the right side of things, mostly."

"He loves me, doesn't he?"

"I wouldn't go that far. He said you were okay but that you attract dead bodies like blowflies to a rotting corpse. Chang says you bring him so many murders to investigate that he doesn't have time to look for any of his own."

"It's a gift, Detective. People with gunshot wounds or knives sticking in them just seem to fall dead at my feet. I find dead people."

"When you didn't show up for our appointment, I dropped by to see if you had left town."

"Sorry, I overslept."

"Well, let's go find a cup of coffee and talk about things."

"You wouldn't want to get coffee here, Detective. They don't have any jelly donuts. I already checked."

"That's okay. Let's get the coffee, anyway. I insist."

"But my car..."

"I'll have the valet hold it here for you. This won't take long."

Reluctantly, I followed Richardson out to the Del's beachfront food truck and bar trailer. I had planned to skip breakfast because I was in a hurry. But since I was a captive audience, I ordered eggs, bacon, and pancakes with my coffee. Richardson got coffee and a breakfast sandwich. We carried our food to a table that overlooked the beach.

"I checked out the guy who died in your room," Richardson said between bites. "His name was Albert Brooks. He arrived in San Diego yesterday afternoon on a flight from New York City."

"A New Yorker, huh?"

"No, he lived here in San Diego and owned a business that deals in antiques and such. I talked to a security guard at his office building this morning and he said Brooks had been in New York to bid on something at a Manhattan auction house."

"He have any employees?" I asked, figuring if my Mission Bay business names theory didn't pan out, maybe I could learn something at Brooks' office.

"Just one," Richardson said, consulting his memo book. "A woman named Sybil Chase. I had the security guard let me in to look for a contact number for her, but we found her in the office."

"What did she have to say?"

"Not much. She was too dead to tell me anything."

"Uh-huh. Well, it was nice talking with you informally like this, Detective. Now, can you just give me a parking ticket or something and let me collect my rental car?"

"Got a date?"

"Yeah. Something like that."

"You should be more careful about the people you're keeping company with, Bishop. Another beating like that and you could end up in a freezer drawer at the coroner's office. And you would make one ugly corpse."

"Then you could tell everybody I was your twin brother."

MY HEAD HURT TOO MUCH to decipher which business might seem more likely than the others, and I just planned on taking them one by one as I got to them. I arrived at the first one, Mission Bay Baja Restaurant, forty minutes after leaving the hotel. I parked across the street from the mostly empty lot and did everything but walk backwards to look like I wasn't going there. After looking the place over and checking for a tail, I went in through the front doors. A young, dark-haired man walked over to me.

"I'm sorry, Señor, but we haven't opened for lunch yet," he said with an accent.

"That's all right," I said. "I'm Bishop and I'm here for the lei niho palaoa."

"Pardon."

"The lei niho palaoa."

"I don't believe..."

"A man named Brooks left it here for me."

"Brooks? Lay... whatever you said?"

"You know, Albert Brooks, the antiquities dealer."

"Antiquities?"

"Yeah, he told me he left the lei niho palaoa here for me. It's about this long and this wide." I pantomimed the approximate dimensions. "It's a plaited human hair necklace and has a sperm whale tooth carved into a hook as the pendant."

"Well, Señor, you can look around, but you can bet we have nothing like that here."

"It's an antique."

"A what?"

"Antique. An ancient, rare artifact that's valuable to collectors and museums."

"You've been in a fight, huh, Señor?"

"Yeah... something like that... now look..."

"You got hit in the head pretty hard, huh?"

"You haven't got the lei niho palaoa?"

"Oh, sure... sure..."

"You have?"

"Sure, we have them with red sauce and green sauce, right out in the kitchen. We're going to have them for lunch."

"Okay..."

"But I don't think we have the one you're looking for. Ours have no hair on them. The food inspectors would frown about that."

"Well, muchas gracias, amigo," I said. "Adios."

That took care of the first bet. I had only six more businesses to check. As I walked out of the restaurant, I made up my mind. If none of the businesses paid off, I was going to get on a plane back to Honolulu and cry myself to sleep every night until I got over the loss of the five thousand dollar bonus.

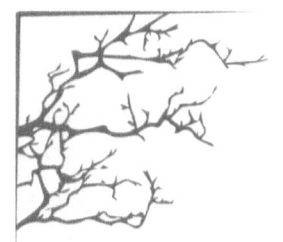

Chapter 9

MISSION BAY BREWING Company was next on my list. I pulled the rental into the parking lot in front of a three-story brick building that looked like it had been around for a while. It had. Raised lettering on the spandrel between the second and third floors said "Established 1932" after the company's name. I parked and went inside the double glass doors. I followed the arrows down a corridor, pointing to the tasting room.

The room layout looked like a usual bar, tables and chairs, and a large wooden bar at the front. There were couples and groups sitting at several tables inside and others at tables outside on the outdoor seating area that I could see through a glass door. I noticed people were not only drinking beer, but were also eating. Above the bar, I spied a poster that showed the tasting room served foods of various cuisines they rotated each day of the week, Monday through Friday. It was Thursday, Mexican cuisine day, according to the poster.

I grabbed a stool at the bar. A young strawberry blonde with freckles on her nose and a welcoming smile came over to take my order. I chose the Mexican style lager from the menu board and a basket of tacos.

She put in my food order and brought me the beer.

"Worked here long?" I asked.

"Almost two years."

"Do you guys get regulars in here, sort of like bars?"

"Some. But we get tourists mostly in town to go to Sea World or to catch a Padres game. Like that."

"Do you know a guy named Albert Brooks, sort of heavyset, gray hair, probably around sixty?"

"No, doesn't sound familiar. Why?"

"He was a guy I did business with. Albert was a little forgetful. He would go in to a restaurant or somewhere and then walk out without his briefcase, eyeglasses, or phone. Sadly, he died suddenly yesterday."

"Oh, no. I'm so sorry."

"It's okay. We weren't really close. Thing is, Albert was supposed to deliver a package he picked up for me in New York City earlier this week. But he didn't have it when he died. I thought maybe he walked off and left it somewhere."

"Hang on a second. Your food is ready."

The woman came back a minute later with the tacos.

"You think the guy came in here?"

"Not necessarily. All I have to go on is he was at some business with Mission Bay in the name. So, I'm just checking all those businesses in the area."

"Huh, I bet there must be a half dozen businesses in the area with Mission Bay in the name, counting us."

I pulled out my memo book and showed it to her. I had already crossed out the restaurant I had visited.

"Seven that I've come up with."

She looked at the list and handed the book back.

"Yes, I can't think of any others. What is it you're looking for?"

"It's an antique," I said. "But it's probably inside a box." I held up my hands. "Probably about this long and this wide."

"People sometimes leave stuff here," she said. "Mostly jackets, umbrellas, a phone occasionally. We store it in the office behind the bar in case the owner comes back for it. But I've never seen anything like what you've described."

"Okay, thanks for the help," I said.

I had already wolfed down the tacos, and I drank the last swallow of beer.

"I didn't really expect to find it here, but I wanted to try the beer and thought I'd stop in."

"Do you have a card or something?"

"Sure," I said, digging a business card out of my wallet. I slid it across the bar.

"A private investigator from Hawaii?"

"Yes, I was supposed to meet Albert yesterday and fly home today. I may be here a little longer than I planned."

"Well, I'll talk to the other employees, and if your package should turn up, I'll call you."

"I appreciate it," I said, standing up. "Thanks again."

"No problem. Thanks for stopping by. I hope you enjoyed the beer."

After paying, I said goodbye and I followed the corridor back to the front doors and went out. As I crossed the parking lot, I spotted a white sedan across the lot with two guys in the front seat who looked like they were trying hard to look like they weren't watching me. I got in the rental and drove out of the lot, turning left onto the street in front of the brewery. A moment later, watching the mirror, I saw the white sedan make a left out of the parking lot. It looked like I had grown a tail.

After I made several random turns, the white sedan continued following, staying two to three cars back. Back on a major thoroughfare, up ahead I saw the traffic light at the next intersection turn green. Continuing to drive the posted speed limit, I knew I would make it through the intersection easily. So, I slowed down.

Checking the mirror, I saw the white sedan was three cars back. As I approached the intersection, the traffic light turned yellow. I braked as if I was going to stop and then, at the last minute, punched the accelerator and entered the intersection just as the light turned red. The driver behind blared his horn at me as he followed me through the intersection. Looking back again, I saw the white sedan had got stuck at the red light behind the two other cars.

Immediately, I turned right onto a side street, followed it two blocks, and made another right turn. Then I drove back in the direction I had come from, continuing to parallel the major thoroughfare I had been on. After several blocks, I turned right again, which brought me back to the thoroughfare. The white sedan was nowhere in sight. So, I continued on until I found the street that would take me to my next destination, Mission Bay Graphics.

Bryan had been the only person I had seen inside the building with Andrew Weismann and had felt concern he might follow me. But I figured the two guys in the white sedan must also be working for Weismann. No one else knew what I was looking for, where I was looking for it, or even why I was in San Diego. I hadn't even told Richardson any of it.

The guys in the sedan must have been following me ever since I had left the hotel. That was the only way they could have followed me to the brewery, unless someone had put a tracker on my car. I decided to check that before I got to the graphics company. I didn't want to make it easy for them to pick me up again.

I turned into a Ralphs Grocery Store parking lot and found a spot with only a few other cars close by. Getting out, I took off my suit jacket and left it on the seat. There are plenty of different devices available for tracking vehicles. Most have magnets to hold them in place and are battery operated. Having used them myself, I knew from experience the most likely places people attached them to cars.

Lying on my back, I stuck my head under the car and checked all the usual locations, but found nothing suspicious. I doubted Bryan had put a GPS tag inside my clothing because the range was too limited to be effective.

Looking at my watch, I saw I had already missed my morning flight back to Honolulu, and unless I got my stay extended at the Hotel Del Coronado, I would not have a hotel room there for the night. While I could just get a room somewhere else, my luggage was still there in my room. I needed to check in with my client before continuing to chase the missing artifact.

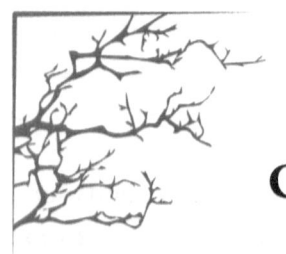

Chapter 10

SITTING IN THE RENTAL in the grocery store parking lot, I called Laurence O'Donnell in Honolulu. O'Donnell picked up right away.

"Hello?"

"Mr. O'Donnell, Richard Bishop here."

"Bishop? It's about time you reported in. Are you calling from the plane?"

"I'm still in San Diego."

"What? Why? Do you have the package?"

"Not at the moment. Brooks failed to deliver."

"What do you mean, he failed to deliver? He phoned me when he arrived back in San Diego with the artifact and was on the way to contact you."

"He showed up at Hotel Del Coronado, but he didn't bring the package with him. Then he had the audacity to die on my hotel room floor."

"What happened?"

"He got himself shot in the back, probably by someone working for Weismann."

"Good lord."

"It's not as bad as it sounds. Not yet, anyway. I have a rough idea of where the artifact is. I'm chasing it down now."

"A rough idea is not good enough for me, Bishop. When I hire a man, I expect him to deliver exactly what I order. And just what do you mean by a rough idea?"

"Before he died, Brooks told me to go to Mission Bay, but he didn't finish the sentence before he expired. I think when he realized someone had followed him from the airport, he ditched the package somewhere to keep them from getting it. Unfortunately, sometime between ditching it and showing up at my hotel room, someone put a bullet in his back."

"Mission Bay? You're speaking of the waterway there?"

"No, I'm referring to the neighborhood centered on its namesake waterway. My theory is that Brooks must have hidden the package inside some business with Mission Bay as a prominent part of its name. That's the only thing that makes sense to me. I'm calling to see what you want done because if I'm to stay on the job we need to work out the logistics."

"I want you to find the lei niho palaoa and bring it here to me in Honolulu. How much simpler do you want it, Bishop?"

"I'm not asking for simplicity, Mr. O'Donnell. I'm asking for you to call and allow Hotel Del Coronado to extend my stay there and to book me a new return flight to Honolulu if you want me to keep looking for the lei niho palaoa."

"Of course I want you to keep looking for it, Mr. Bishop."

"Then you will take care of the hotel and flight arrangements?"

"I just knew I had picked a clever person who makes good decisions," O'Donnell said unpleasantly. "I think I've already paid for an ample stay at an expensive hotel for you to accomplish what I hired you to do. And I already paid for your round-trip airfare. I fail to see why I should pay additional expenses resulting from your incompetent handling of a simple assignment."

"Mr. O'Donnell, it's hardly my fault your courier failed to show up with the package in hand, got himself shot, and then impolitely died before telling me exactly where he left the artifact. If you don't want to make good on the expenses, fine. I'll grab the next flight back to Honolulu and you can just kiss the lei niho palaoa goodbye."

"Don't be impertinent, Mr. Bishop. I want that artifact found and delivered to me."

"Look, since I arrived here, a big ugly guy sapped me, kidnapped me, and beat me half to death after tying me to a chair. I'm already feeling a little disenchanted with this job. You want me to be happy in my work, don't you, Mr. O'Donnell? If so, I need you to extend my hotel stay and book me another flight."

"It's Thursday. I will extend your stay at the hotel through Saturday evening. I will also book you on a Sunday morning flight back to Honolulu. After that, if you haven't found the artifact by Sunday morning, I'll make other arrangements."

"Okay, Mr. O'Donnell."

"Good afternoon, then," O'Donnell said, and then he disconnected.

Suddenly, a thought occurred to me. Mission Bay wasn't such a large place that those guys in the white sedan couldn't find me again if they worked hard enough at it. Weismann had told me that Bryan had followed me from Honolulu to San Diego and he had probably watched me drive the rental out of the agency's airport lot. I needed alternative transportation before proceeding on my quest. It made sense to leave the rental in the parking lot temporarily, as I didn't want to waste time driving it back to the airport to switch to a different car. I took out my phone, searched for Uber and then called for a pickup.

THE UBER DRIVER, WHO looked like a Pakistani, arrived in a gray Prius. I was waiting in front of the store. I got in and gave him the address for Mission Bay Graphics. Ten minutes later, the driver turned into the parking lot of a tired strip mall. I saw the company sign, but something about the place didn't feel right, so I asked the driver to wait instead of paying him and sending him on his way.

As I approached the entrance of the business, I saw a large sign in the window advertising the space was available for lease. Cupping my hands against the front door, I peered inside through the dusty glass and found the space dark and empty. No people, no furnishings, nada. It seemed Mission Bay Graphics had either gone out of business or moved to another location. It looked like the business had vacated the premises months before. Taking out my phone, I called the number for the business I had jotted down in my memo book. After three rings, a recording told me the number had been disconnected or was no longer in service. I scratched Mission Bay Graphics off my list, which left me with only four more candidates to check.

After I gave the driver another address, he drove me to Mission Bay Appliances, located in another strip mall. When we got there, a sign in the door told me the business was closed for the day and invited me to call again. Riding around in a car all day hadn't helped my stiff, sore body, and it was late afternoon. Since I had two more full days to search, I called it quits and told the driver to take me back to the grocery store. There I paid him, retrieved the rental and drove back to the hotel. To my disappointment, Detective Richardson was waiting for me in the lobby and he followed me, without invitation, up to my room.

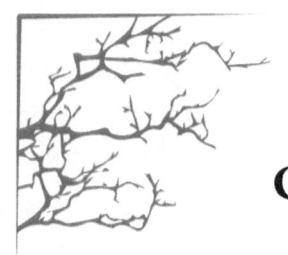

Chapter 11

WE WENT INSIDE. I CLOSED the door and then glared at Richardson.

"What is it now, Detective?" I asked.

"Bishop, maybe you have done nothing yet that I can prove and arrest you for, but it doesn't mean I'm not keeping an eye on you."

"Your concern is touching, Detective, but I don't need you to look after me."

"I'm not looking after you, Bishop. You know how many homicides we had in Coronado last year?"

"No, but I have a feeling you're going to tell me."

"None, that's how many. You know how many homicides we've had this year?"

"No idea."

"One. That means homicides are up one hundred percent since you arrived in our little city, Bishop. And the chief doesn't want you adding to the total. And neither does San Diego PD, for that matter."

"It's hardly my fault, Detective. I came here to the San Diego area because I'd heard it was much safer than LA, and I was looking for a nice, quiet vacation. Yet it seems I have walked right into a crime wave. What kind of city are you running here, anyway?"

Richardson shook his head. "You still haven't told me what you're doing in Coronado, Bishop. Considering the beating someone already gave you, if you level with me, maybe we can help each other. Maybe we have no more murders and you won't get beaten to death."

"I didn't plan on any of it, Detective. I came here to do a simple job and was supposed to be on a flight back to Honolulu this morning."

"So why didn't you make the flight? The desk clerk just told me you extended your stay through the weekend. And drop the gag. How did you know Albert Brooks?"

I sighed, but couldn't think of a good reason not to tell the nice policeman.

"I'm on a case he was involved in."

"What case?"

"He was supposed to deliver a rare, old, and expensive cultural artifact to me, which I was supposed to take back to my client in Honolulu."

"What kind of artifact?"

"If it was pertinent, I'd tell you."

"If I want to know, you will tell me," Richardson said in a tone as sharp and flat as sheet metal. "I'm quickly losing patience with you, Bishop."

"I don't make a living telling cops everything they want to know about a client's business."

"I don't make a living taking crap from shyster private detectives like you, Bishop. You're working my side of the street in my town and if you get in my way, I'll put you in jail. Got it?"

"Can I feel your muscle?" I asked.

"Keep it up, Bishop, and you will look like you went through a coffee grinder."

"Now I won't be able to sleep without a night light burning."

Richardson shrugged. "All right, have it your way, Bishop. But I will stick to you closer than your shadow until you're on a plane out of here."

"Are you mad at me, Detective?"

"How could anyone get mad at a sweetheart like you?"

"Okay, I'll level with you. My client, a dealer in rare antiquities, hired me to come here to pick up a Hawaiian cultural artifact called a lei niho palaoa. It's a necklace made of plaited human hair with a hook-shaped pendant carved from the tooth of a whale. Important people, like chiefs in ancient Hawaii, wore the necklaces as a sign of their rank. Albert Brooks was supposed to deliver the artifact to me here so I could deliver to my client in Honolulu. But when Brooks showed up here, all he brought with him was the slug in his back."

"So why would someone kill Brooks over a necklace made of hair? Is it valuable?"

"The original owner of the necklace, a famous Hawaiian chief, makes the necklace both rare and valuable to private collectors and museums. My client says he wanted to repatriate the necklace and hand it over to a museum in Honolulu. But there is another dealer here in San Diego who also wants to gain possession of it. I believe someone in his employ shot Albert Brooks."

"Who is this rival dealer?"

"His name is Weismann. Andrew Weismann. And he has a slugger named Bryan, who also packs a large frame semi-automatic, working for him. I figure Bryan put the bullet in Brooks. He also slugged me with the gun outside the hotel, knocking me unconscious, and took me out to what looked like a large metal farm building somewhere outside town where I met Weismann. They had tied me to a chair inside the building and Bryan beat the stuffing out of me to encourage me to tell them where the necklace was."

"But you didn't know where it was?"

"No, I still don't. They finally determined I didn't know, so they let me go, figuring they could follow me around until I led them to it so they could take it from me if I recovered it."

"This Bryan have a last name?"

"Probably. Most people do. But I don't know what it is."

"San Diego is a big place. If they believed you didn't know where it was, what makes them think you will find the necklace?"

"They think Brooks might have told me where he stashed it before he died."

"Did he?"

"Not exactly. He tried, but only got part of it out before he died."

"What did he say?"

"That I will not share with you, Detective."

"Don't be an idiot, Bishop. We could probably find it faster than you can and maybe Weismann's goon won't ice you in the process."

"I don't want the cops involved. Right now, the police have no interest in the necklace. It isn't evidence. But if the police recover it, it will be in a property room gathering dust. I would return to Honolulu without it, and I would miss out on a generous fee."

Richardson shook his head again, clearly not pleased.

"Well, I can't force you to tell me," he said finally. Then he turned and walked to the door.

I followed and held the door open for him, and he went out. But he stopped and turned back to me.

"It would be easier for everyone and safer for you to let us take over recovering the necklace. Yes, we would hold on to it for a while. But as long as your client has proof of ownership, we would give it to him eventually. I want you to think about what I'm telling you."

"I certainly will give it some thought, Detective," I said.

Satisfied he had got through to me, Richardson turned and walked toward the elevator.

"But don't worry," I called after him. "I'll take it from here, Detective." Then I closed the door.

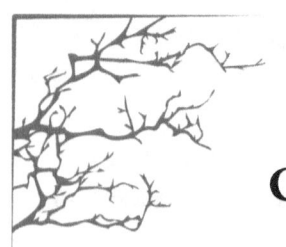

Chapter 12

AT 11:00 A.M., FRIDAY morning, another Uber driver picked me up in front of the hotel. I had stayed in my room the evening before, after Richardson had left. Instead of going downstairs for dinner and drinks, I had ordered a pizza and a six-pack of beer from room service. I hadn't wanted to risk running into Marlee Martin in a hotel restaurant or bar. Sure, I liked her, but that was the problem. I hadn't seen Sally in three days, and spending more time with Marlee was more of a temptation than I needed to risk.

When we left Hotel Del Coronado and crossed the bridge into San Diego, I had the driver do a one-hour surveillance detection route or SDR, a fancy term used by intelligence operatives for a tactic used to determine if someone was following either on foot or in a vehicle.

An SDR incorporated three elements: distance, time, and change of direction. The distance concept was simple. If you noticed a car was behind you over a long distance, then you could believe that car might be a tail. But that was only one piece of the puzzle.

The longer distance you traveled, the higher the likelihood that a car following you would stand out, since you have more time to notice it if you are paying attention. Unless multiple vehicles were tailing you, seeing the same car for an extended time would set off some warning bells in your brain. Again, alone, the time test was only a part of the puzzle.

Changing your direction of travel helped avoid the random "going in the same direction" or "out driving around town at the same time" random event. The more changes of direction you incorporated, the better chance you had of detecting a tail. If going from Point A to Point B comprised six turns and the same vehicle was behind you for each of them, you had more confidence the car was following you. That said, the test, like the others, could produce false detections if used alone. But incorporating all three could help you identify a tail.

After an hour, I had observed no suspicious vehicles and gave the driver the address for my first stop of the morning, Mission Bay Moving & Storage. Had I prioritized my list before starting, the moving and storage company might have been first on my list. And I figured it would be a simple place to rule in or out. I doubted Brooks would have left the package with someone at the office. He would have rented a storage unit.

When we arrived, I paid the driver and sent him away. I planned on using a different Uber for each stop during the day to make it harder for Weismann's minions to locate and follow me from destination to destination.

When I walked in, I found an older, balding man sitting behind the counter.

"Help you?" he asked.

"Yes, my name is David DuBois," I said, digging in my wallet.

I produced a fake business card, one from a stack a print shop in Honolulu had printed for me, which I used when working undercover. It identified me as David DuBois, attorney at law.

"I'm an attorney representing the estate of Albert Brooks."

The man looked at the business card.

"You're from Honolulu, Hawaii?"

"That's right," I said, wishing I had some fake San Diego attorney business cards. The guy was sharper than he looked.

"Mr. Brooks passed away unexpectedly this week and I'm completing an inventory of his property for probate. I understand he has a storage unit rented here, and I need to access it and inventory the contents."

"Why would an attorney come all the way here from Hawaii for something like this? We have lots of attorneys right here in San Diego."

"Of course," I said. "But Mr. Brooks split his time between San Diego and Honolulu and actually had more extensive real estate holdings in Hawaii than California. That's why my firm is handling the estate."

"Well, don't you need a court order or something? I don't think I can let you enter someone's storage unit unless you have something in writing from the court. For one thing, I would have to cut the lock."

"I applaud your commitment to safeguarding your customer's property," I said. "But I don't wish to remove anything from the unit. I only wish to inventory the contents. And, of course, I'm happy to pay you for a replacement lock to re-secure the unit when I've finished."

"Well, I would have to witness everything," the man said, seeming to weaken. "I couldn't just turn you loose in someone's storage unit alone."

"More than acceptable," I said.

"Okay, what did you say the name was again?"

"Brooks. Albert Brooks."

The man typed on the keyboard of an ancient-looking Dell desktop. His brow furrowed in consternation. Then, after several minutes, he looked up at me.

"I guess someone misinformed you," he said. "We have no Albert Brooks listed as a storage unit renter. You sure this is the right place?"

"Perhaps it's rented under his first initial and last name," I suggested. "Mr. Brooks sometimes did that."

The man looked at the screen again.

"Nope, we have no Brooks listed at all."

"All right, thank you," I said. "Sorry to trouble you."

I turned and left. Every storage unit rental company I had ever dealt with required identification with a photo before renting to someone, so I doubted Brooks had rented a unit under an alias. I felt sure I could scratch the moving and rental company off my list even though I had arrived with high hopes.

I waited twenty minutes in front of Mission Bay Moving & Storage for another Uber driver to pick me up. Getting in the back, I gave her the address for Mission Bay Appliances. I had noticed on the door sign the previous day the business opened at 9:00 a.m. and would be open when we arrived.

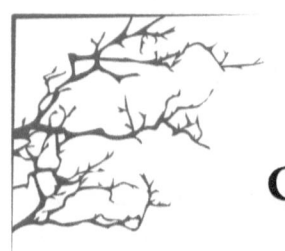

Chapter 13

WALKING INTO THE APPLIANCE store, I groaned inwardly. Unless an acquaintance of Brooks worked here, he had entrusted the package to, he might have just walked in off the street and stashed it in one of the display appliances on the floor. And I saw dozens and dozens of appliances I would have to look inside of for the package. A middle-aged sales clerk with a name tag identifying him as Dan approached me.

"How can we help you today?" Dan asked with a friendly smile.

"I just bought a house in the area," I said. "Since I'm moving from an apartment with all the appliances included, I'm going to need to buy appliances for the house."

"What are you looking for?" Dan asked, rubbing his hands together in anticipation of a big sale.

"Range, refrigerator, washer and dryer. The works. The house has a dishwasher, but it looks old, so I might also be in the market for one of those."

"Well, you came to the right place, Mr...."

"Bishop. Rick Bishop."

"We have the best prices on the highest quality appliances in San Diego," Dan said. "None of those big box store rejects here. No, sir. We sell appliances that last and will give you years of trouble-free service."

"Sounds like what I'm looking for," I said.

"We also offer flexible financing at great rates if you need it."

"Yes, since I need everything, I could probably use the financing."

"Can I ask how you heard about us, Mr. Bishop? The owner always wants us to ask to see which advertising channel is giving us the biggest bang for the buck."

"I understand," I said. "But actually, a good friend recommended you. He buys all his appliances here."

"Is that right? What's his name? We surely want to thank him for telling his friends about us."

"Albert Brooks. You probably know him if you have been with the store for long."

"Hm," Dan said, scratching his chin. "Albert Brooks? I can't say the name sounds familiar. And I've worked here for almost nine years."

"Well, Dan, like you said, you sell appliances offering years of trouble-free service, so Al may not have been in for a while. All I know is he spoke very highly of the store and told me he gets all his appliances here."

"That's just great," Dan beamed. "I'll have to check the customer records later and send him out a discount coupon for his next purchase. Now, what would you like to look at first?"

I scanned the floor, wondering which appliance might have caught Brooks' eye if he had stashed the package here. It seemed clear Dan wasn't a friend Brooks had asked to hold the package for him. And when I had given Dan my name, he hadn't reacted to it at all. Surely, Brooks would have told anyone he left the package with the name of the person who would come for it.

"Well, I suppose I would like to see the ranges first," I said.

"Right this way, Mr. Bishop," Dan said, leading the way.

"Any particular color, finish, or style you're interested in?" he asked.

"No, I'm open-minded," I said. "I'm more interested in the oven size. I do a lot of cooking at home and definitely want an oven that can handle a full size bird next Thanksgiving."

"Well, let's take a look at what we have."

I followed Dan down a long row of ranges, some natural gas, and some electric models. I assured him I had hookups for both available and wasn't sold on one over the other. He pulled open the oven doors and rattled on about the features of each range. Each one proved empty. If Brooks had been here, he hadn't left the package in a range. I figured Dan's arm was getting tired from yanking open oven doors by the time we looked inside every oven on the sales floor.

Looking around, it occurred to me that Brooks would have probably chosen an appliance near the front doors to avoid someone like Dan intercepting him when he wanted a few seconds of privacy. So, once we finished with ovens, I pointed at the washers and dryers lined up at the front to either side of the front doors.

"You know, Dan, why don't you just let me browse the washers and dryers?" I said. "I'm sure you have other stuff to do, and to be honest, I'm a guy who takes his time before deciding on important purchases."

"You sure?" Dan asked. "I don't mind showing you the features and all. Heck, that's my job."

"No, I'll go it alone and I'll come find you if I have questions."

"Well, all right, if you're sure."

Dan left me looking a little dejected. Without him holding me back like a boat anchor, I made quick work of the dozens of washers and dryers. Again, as I closed the last dryer door, I swallowed my disappointment. I moved to the refrigerator section as stealthily as possible, hoping to avoid attracting Dan's attention.

I had checked every refrigerator and was halfway through the dishwashers when Dan tracked me down.

"Find anything you like?" Dan asked cheerfully.

"Yes, but I'm still looking at dishwashers. I might as well replace the older model in the house while I'm buying. Start with everything new."

"That's a wise decision," Dan agreed, giving me a friendly slap on the back.

Meanwhile, I kept moving down the row of dishwashers, desperate the find the object of my search. But it was not to be. With Dan talking non-stop, I came to the last one and found it empty except for the trays you loaded dishes in for cleaning.

"Are you ready to write up an order?" Dan asked. "We rarely do this, but I'm going to throw in free delivery."

"That's swell of you, Dan," I said. "I've selected the appliances I really like, but you know how it is. I'll have to bring the little woman in and get her input. She is at work today, but since it's my day off, I just thought I'd come in first and look myself."

"Oh, sure," Dan sounding even more deflated than when I asked to browse without his help. "When do you think you and the wife will be back in?"

"Are you open tomorrow?" I asked.

"Yes, sir. Nine to five."

"You working tomorrow, Dan?" I asked.

"You bet."

"Swell, you've been so helpful today, I wouldn't want anyone else to help us."

Dan rubbed his hands together again.

"I appreciate that, Mr. Bishop. Looking forward to seeing you tomorrow and meeting Mrs. Bishop."

I thanked Dan profusely, feeling a little bad he would never see me again or have the chance to meet the imaginary Mrs. Bishop. But what I felt worse about was hitting another dry hole.

Waiting outside on my third Uber of the day, I scratched a line through the appliance store. I had two possibilities left. The paving company and Mission Bay Bolt & Nut, which I assumed must be a hardware store.

Having wasted so much time at the appliances store, I felt I only had time to check one of them and would have to save the last one for tomorrow morning if it became necessary. I really thought the hardware store was the best possibility of the two. I knew little about paving companies, but pictured a big gravel lot with one tiny office building in the middle. Of course, there would probably be lots of heavy equipment someone could hide a small package inside.

The Uber arrived. I got in and gave him the address for Mission Bay Bolt & Nut.

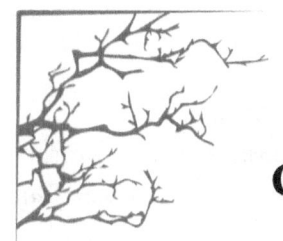

Chapter 14

MISSION BAY BOLT & Nut was all the way on the other side of the neighborhood on a street inside an industrial park. The Uber driver dropped me off out front, and I walked to the front door. A guy standing on the other side flipped the "We're Open" sign to "Sorry We're Closed" and locked the door just as I reached it. It was 4:01 p.m. by my watch and even though the business hours on the door said 7:00 a.m. to 4 p.m., I thought that was rude. I banged on the glass door with my open palm. The guy unlocked the door and opened it a crack.

"We're closed," he said. "Come back tomorrow."

"Albert sent me," I said.

"Beat it," the man said, closing the door.

I had missed lunch and was in a foul mood. I shoved the door open and pushed my way inside.

"Hey, what do you think you're doing? I told you..."

"Don't talk," I said menacingly. "Just listen. A guy named O'Donnell sent me to San Diego to meet a guy named Albert Brooks. Brooks was supposed to give me a package, but he got killed."

"What?" the guy said, his eyes opened wide.

"Yeah, and just before he died, Albert said Mission Bay. Now, if this is the place he meant for me to come for the package, say so. I missed lunch and I'm on my last nerve."

"Albert is dead?" the man gasped.

"Oh. You know him?"

"He's my brother. Come in and shut the door."

"Look, I'm sorry that I just blurted it out that your brother was dead like that. I didn't know he was your brother. But you've got the package?"

"What's your name?"

"Bishop. Rick Bishop."

"Yeah, Albert said you would be by and you fit the description he gave me. I'm Stanley Brooks. What happened to my brother?"

"Someone who wanted to intercept the package shot him. He was bad off when he came to my hotel room and died about a minute after he walked inside."

"Okay. Well, the package is in the back. Follow me."

I followed Stanley to the back of the store. He reached into an open crate of ten-penny nails, fished around for a few moments, and then pulled out a rectangular package wrapped in brown paper and tied with string. He turned to hand it to me, but when I reached out for it, he froze.

"Don't move, either of you," a familiar voice said.

"Who is this guy?" Stanley asked.

I already knew who had spoken, but turned my head to look.

"Oh, his name is Bryan. He likes to tie people to chairs and beat them up."

I turned to face Bryan. He had his big gun pointed at me.

"I won't beat you up this time, Bishop. You shouldn't have lied to Mr. Weismann. I'll have to kill you for it."

"This is probably the guy who killed your brother," I said to Stanley.

"Yeah?"

I noticed in my peripheral vision that Stanley's eyes were flitting from Bryan to a row of shovels hanging on the wall and back again. I knew he might be our only chance because I was too far from the rack. Even if he wasn't fast enough to grab and swing a shovel at him before getting shot, the distraction might at least give me the chance to jump Bryan.

"Give me the package," Bryan growled.

"You killed, Albert, huh?"

Bryan shifted the muzzle of the gun to Stanley.

"Don't make me tell you again," he said. "Give me the package."

Stanley held it out towards him.

"Just toss it over here."

Stanley launched the package at Bryan's face like a guard at the top of the key, hitting a post man under the basket with a crisp two-handed pass. Bryan instinctively raised his right forearm to ward it off. Stanley had already seized a shovel from the rack and had swung it at Bryan like a batter swinging at a high fastball by the time the package bounced off Bryan's raised forearm. But Bryan recovered quickly, extended his right arm and shot Stanley as the flat side of the shovel blade arced toward him.

Stanley was a gamer and hadn't stopped the swing. It smacked Bryan's extended fist on the follow through and the pistol flew out of his hand. At the same instant, I drove my shoulder into Bryan's chest like a safety, spearing a wide receiver after a catch, knocking Bryan against a beam support column.

I heard the air whoosh out of his lungs. I grabbed him by the right upper arm, spun him around, and launched him toward the nail crate. His stomach slammed down on top of it and then he rolled onto his back, trying to get up.

Then I jumped on him and grabbed his neck with both hands, trying to choke him out. But Bryan was strong. He pushed back and got back on his feet. He got his hands around my throat. I foot swept him and he fell back onto the crate and I slammed his head against the edge a couple of times.

He got his right foot up and against my gut, extended his leg, and I flew backward, landing on my butt on the floor. He grabbed a pair of garden shears from a display and tried to stab me as I got back up. I got a grip on his right wrist with both hands and slammed his fist against the beam support until I dislodged the shears from his hand. Then I grabbed a handful of his suit jacket with my right hand, grabbed him by the neck with my left hand, and slammed him face first into the post.

We both fell to the floor, but jumped back to our feet. He bum-rushed me and drove his shoulder into my gut, wrapping his arms around my waist. He shoved me backwards until I crashed into some sturdy wood shelving.

I drove my right knee into his gut twice, forcing him to stand up, and then grabbed him by the lapels and drove him backwards into another row of shelves. I took a step back, loading up a straight right, but Bryan beat me to the punch with a right hook. My shoulder absorbed most of it, but it still hurt and I fell back into a gardening display. Bryan launched at me just as my left hand found the handle of a metal watering can. I swung it and clocked him on the right side of the head, taking the starch out of his momentum.

The blow stunned him, but didn't put him down and I lost my grip on the handle when the can connected. I grabbed a handful of his jacket with my left hand and punched him in the face with my right. His head snapped back and gripping his jacket with both hands, I drove him backwards across the floor until his back hit a plate glass window. The window shattered. He went out backwards but had a grip on my jacket and pulled me through the window after him.

We both slammed onto the concrete sidewalk in front of the building, Bryan on his right side and me on my left. The fall stunned us both, and we lay still for a beat before we rolled toward each other with fists flying. Somehow, I got on top of him with him flat on his back. I had my right forearm pressed against his throat and I punched him twice with my left hand. Then I grabbed him by the throat and choked him again until he stopped resisting. Then I raised up and pummeled him again and again with both fists.

The window had been old-fashioned plate glass, not safety glass. I felt Bryan shifting beneath me and realized he was stretching out his right hand, trying to grab a wicked-looking shard of broken glass to use as a weapon. I grabbed his throat again and pressed my weight down on him to prevent him from reaching for the glass. But then he punched me with a solid shot to the right kidney and my entire right side went numb. I tumbled off him to the left. Bryan rolled to the right and snatched up the glass shard he had struggled to reach.

I rolled left to get away from him, but hit the side of the building and came to rest on my back. Bryan sprang on top of me like a cat. With his knees straddling my chest, and the shard in both hands, he drove the jagged tip downward towards my throat. I gripped his wrists with both my hands to keep the glass shard from stabbing me in the throat. He put all his weight behind his wrists, trying to force the tip toward my throat.

I was losing the fight. When I tried desperately to squirm out from under him, I lost my grip with my right hand for an instant and he fell forward to his left and the tip of the glass shard plunged into the right side of my abdomen.

Frantically, I ran my right hand over the sidewalk and found a shard of my own and drove it into the inside of his right thigh. Bryan shrieked and raised up, and I shoved him away and rolled out from under him. He fell off me to my left. I got to my knees and pulled the shard of glass out of my abdomen, and tried to stand, expecting another attack. But to my surprise, Bryan was limping as fast as he could toward his gray sedan in the parking lot.

I lurched after him, but fell to my hands and knees just as he got in the car. He started it, yanked the wheel hard left, and with squealing tires the car shot out of the lot, fishtailed into the street, and drove away.

I got back to my feet, feeling faint, and bleeding like a stuck pig. I staggered back through the front door. After grabbing a rag off the counter, I folded it and pressed it against my stab wound and went to check on Stanley.

He was still lying on his back on the floor moaning, so I knew he wasn't dead. I grabbed a bundle of rags from the paint aisle and knelt beside him. He had taken the bullet in his left shoulder. The act of swinging the shovel had probably saved him from taking it in the center of the chest. I rolled him onto his right side and saw it was a through and through.

Easing him onto his back, I pressed folded rags against the entry wound and stuffed more rags beneath his shoulder to put pressure on the exit wound. Then I dug out my phone and called nine-one-one.

With the San Diego cops and an ambulance on the way, I got up and scoured the floor until I found Bryan's gun. I tucked into my waistband beneath my coat. Then I walked over, and with a groan, picked up the package. I staggered back over to Stanley and sat down on the floor beside him. Then I eased down until I was lying on my back on the floor, clutching the package to my chest.

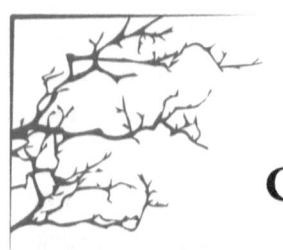

Chapter 15

SATURDAY MORNING, I woke up in bed at Mercy Hospital San Diego. I had lost consciousness briefly before the cops and paramedics arrived at Stanley's hardware store. But I had come around in the ambulance once they had hooked up the IV and started giving me fluids. They had transported me and Stanley in separate ambulances, so I didn't know if they had brought us to the same hospital.

They had rolled me into the emergency room where the nurses removed my jacket and shirt, and the doctor had gone to work irrigating and stitching up my stab wound. Then the medical staff treated my other sundry, but less serious cuts and injuries from going through the glass window with Bryan and absorbing the second beating he had given me. The doctor had told me he was keeping me overnight for observation and that he told the police they would have to wait for my condition to stabilize before he would allow them to question me about what had happened.

When they rolled me into a private room, a nurse gave me a hospital gown to put on. Claiming modesty and being ambulatory, I had gone into the bathroom and shut the door to strip off my bloody slacks and clean up before putting on the gown. They hadn't found the pistol in my back waistband in the emergency room and I had wanted to hang onto it. I had stood on the toilet seat and had hidden the pistol and the package that I had never let go of inside the bathroom drop ceiling.

Since I got enough trouble from Richardson, I had no interest in hanging around the hospital until his San Diego counterparts showed up to question me. I pulled out the IV needle, got out of bed, and went to the door. I opened it a crack, checked the corridor, and found the coast clear.

Slipping out of the room, I hot-footed it down the hallway until I found a staff locker room. There, I found a set of light blue scrubs and beat it back to my room with them. I took off the hospital gown and put on the scrubs, knowing they would have discarded my bloody clothes I'd worn into the emergency room. I found my phone in the drawer of the bedside table and then, opening the closet, I found my shoes and put them on without socks. After retrieving the gun and the package from the bathroom drop ceiling, I was ready to go.

The corridor was still clear, so I hurried down to the fire exit at the end of the hallway and took the stairs down to the ground floor with the pistol back in my waistband covered by the scrub's top and the package under my arm. I followed the signs to the emergency room and slipped out through the ambulance entrance, and walked away from the hospital.

Less than a block from the hospital, I found a McDonald's and ordered a breakfast sandwich, coffee, and orange juice. Given the proximity to the hospital, no one gave me a second glance because of the scrubs I wore. While I ate my breakfast, I called for an Uber.

The Uber driver picked me up in front of the restaurant ten minutes later and I told the driver to take me to the nearest men's clothing store. She drove to a place on West University Avenue. I paid the fare, got out, and went inside. I bought a pair of slacks, a sports coat, two dress shirts, underwear, and socks. Then I went into a changing room, took off the scrubs, and put on the new suit of clothes. I left the scrubs in a trash can and left the store feeling almost human again.

There was a coffee shop down the block I had spotted from the Uber. I headed there because I wanted to get my first look at the contents of the package that had caused me so much misery and wanted to call O'Donnell in Honolulu. After buying a cup of coffee at the counter, I found a table at the back, away from the other customers. I untied the string and unwrapped the box.

When I opened it, I folded back the tissue paper and looked over the lei niho palaoa. I was no expert on cultural artifacts, but it looked like the real deal and was very old. Lifting it out of the box for a closer look, my elbow knocked the box off the table, and besides the sound of the cardboard hitting the floor, I heard something that sounded like a marble bouncing off the tile floor.

Because bending over was painful, I got up and squatted to pick up the box and then spied the object that had sounded like a marble when it hit the floor. I leaned under the table and picked it up. Then I stood, put the box back on the table, and sat back down. In my hand was a whale's tooth carved into the shape of a fishhook. I examined the lei niho palaoa and saw it had a whale tooth pendant identical to the one I held in my hand. That seemed odd. I doubted the ancient Hawaiians had kept spare pendants for their ceremonial necklaces lying around.

Dropping the extra whale's tooth into my jacket pocket, I placed the necklace back into the box and examined the whale tooth pendant closely. Near the top of it, where the pendant attached to the plaited hair necklace, I spotted a tiny line about the width of a hair. The line ran the circumference of the top of the tooth and the perfection of it showed someone had cut or etched the line using a tool the ancient Hawaiians wouldn't have had when they had carved the pendant hundreds of years before.

Taking the extra tooth pendant out of my pocket, I inspected it and found it had no corresponding line around the top. If the lei niho palaoa was authentic, as I believed it was, I speculated the extra pendant was the original and someone had substituted the other pendant for it. Evidently, they had kept the original so they could switch them back again for some unknown reason.

Returning the spare tooth pendant to my pocket, I grasped the pendant attached to the necklace with my fingers at the top and bottom and twisted. The pendant turned in my fingers easily and unscrewed. Once I had separated the hook end from the top, I saw someone had cut female threads into the top portion and male threads at the top of the hook portion and had drilled a cylindrical cavity into the bottom portion of the tooth. I upended it and tapped it lightly on the table. To my surprise, a blood red gemstone clattered onto the table.

While I was no gem expert either, I had seen a similar stone before. A much smaller one-carat stone owned by Sally Jayne Fisher. It was a red diamond, also known as a Fancy Red, according to Sally. She had told me red diamonds were the rarest of the rare and that almost all of them, which came mostly from the Argyle Diamond Mine in Australia, were less than one-carat in weight. From its size, I figured the stone in front of me was at least five-carats in weight. And if it was real, it was probably worth around twenty million dollars.

Although O'Donnell hadn't mentioned the value of the lei niho palaoa, I figured it was worth only a million dollars, if that. And suddenly I understood why people had been willing to kill to get their hands on the lei niho palaoa, the rare gemstone concealed inside the substitute pendant.

I replaced the diamond inside the pendant cavity and screwed the portions back together. Then I put the top back on the box and tied the box with the string. I took out my phone and called Laurence O'Donnell.

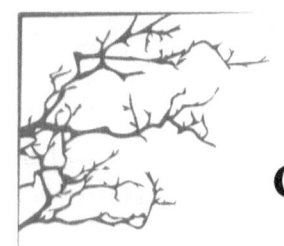

Chapter 16

O'DONNELL MUST HAVE been expecting me to call. He picked up on the first ring.

"Do you have the package yet?"

"We'll get to that," I replied. "I want to ask some questions first."

"Never mind what you do or don't want to know. I want your report right now. What is the status of the package?"

"Let's trade," I said. "You answer my questions and I'll answer yours."

"Your my employee," he snapped. "I don't have to give you any information whatsoever." O'Donnell was acting tough, but beginning to soften around the edges.

"I'm your employee if I want to be, Mr. O'Donnell."

"You accepted the assignment. You took the advance."

"I accepted the assignment, and I completed the assignment. You told me to come here, meet your associate when he contacted me, and to take delivery of the package."

"And to deliver it to me here in Honolulu," he growled. "You haven't completed the assignment until you do so."

"But your associate failed to deliver the package to me, Mr. O'Donnell. Remember? That's where your argument falls apart. That wasn't on me. Me chasing around all over San Diego searching for your package if your associate failed to live up to his part of the bargain was never part of the assignment or our agreement."

"You better watch your step, Bishop."

"You better decide, Mr. O'Donnell, what you wanted when you hired me, while I decide whether I got offered a job or got suckered into a situation I knew nothing about."

"You're pretty stubborn, Bishop."

"I guess, but I have to be in my business. Otherwise, I wouldn't be in business. I've done what I agreed to do for you right up to the point your associate showed up without the package and expired on my hotel room floor. Since then I've endured harassment from the local cops, got sapped, received death threats, and got beaten half to death. Twice now. I've got stabbed, had a gun stuck in my face, and had one of my best suits ruined. All that because I've been searching for your package. And that wasn't even part of the assignment you gave me in Honolulu."

"What is this, Bishop?" he asked angrily. "A shakedown? For more money you will finish the job? That's unethical."

I laughed. "So I have ethics now? Maybe we're finally getting somewhere. But no. I'm not trying to extort you. I just want some answers."

"I still don't like your attitude," he snapped. "But go ahead. Ask your questions. Then I'll decide if I'll answer them."

"Okay, how much is the lei niho palaoa worth?"

"What business is that of yours?"

"The answer bears on my other question."

O'Donnell sighed noisily. "I purchased it at a Manhattan auction for eight hundred thousand dollars."

"That's even less than I thought," I said. "So what is so special about this particular lei niho palaoa? I've seen several fine examples of them at the Bishop Museum. Why is getting this one so important?"

O'Donnell answered as if he was speaking to a dull child. "Because it belonged to King Kalani'opu'u, uncle of Kamehameha. And provenance exists that proves it."

"Okay, but let's return to monetary value. I wouldn't sneeze at eight hundred thousand dollars if someone offered it to me. But I wouldn't kill for it. Someone has already killed for the lei niho palaoa. They will kill again to get it if they have to. And they have tried. Why? Is it because there is much more to it than just a cultural relic with provenance behind it?"

O'Donnell was silent for several moments. "What is it you think you know, Bishop?"

"I don't know anything. That's why I'm asking questions."

"Well, I assume you're asking why Andrew Weismann would kill to get his hands on the lei niho palaoa. I have no idea. Maybe you should ask him if you're so curious about it. I've answered your questions. Now answer mine. Do you have the package?"

I didn't want to tell him, but I knew I had to. I had up to a point accepted the assignment, and giving his money back was the only ethical way to back out now, which I didn't want to do.

"I do," I said.

"That's fine," he said, the relief in his voice palpable. "Make certain you're on the flight tomorrow morning and we will conclude the matter." O'Donnell hung up.

I hadn't really learned anything. What had I expected? That O'Donnell would admit to me he was using a cultural artifact to smuggle a priceless jewel? That left me stumped. What was I going to do? Just carry the package back to Honolulu and get my bonus?

I'd long since finished the coffee and the employees behind the counter kept glancing my way, like they were trying to communicate to me telepathically to either buy something else or move along. Picking up the box, I headed for the door. I dropped the wadded brown paper wrapping in a trash can on my way out.

The Uber I'd called picked me up, and I told the driver to take me back to Hotel Del Coronado.

When the Uber driver dropped me in front of the hotel, I walked inside the lobby and considered briefly consigning the box to the hotel safe, but thought better of it. Instead, I decided I would go up to my room, collect my bag, and then come right back down and check out. I'd find another hotel to spend my last night in San Diego before catching the morning flight to Honolulu. Weismann and his boy, Bryan, knew I had the package and knew where I was staying. I doubted they had given up. The sooner I left the Hotel Del Coronado, the better.

I got on the elevator and rode it up to my room on the fifth floor.

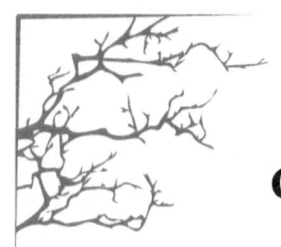

Chapter 17

WHEN I WALKED INTO the room, it was stuffy after being closed up for two days. I didn't plan to be there long, but had to pack my meager belongings. I dropped the package on the foot of the bed, pulled the pistol out of my waistband, and dropped it on the bed beside the box. Then I walked to the balcony door, opened the drapes, and slid open the glass door. When I turned around, Marlee Martin stood framed in the bathroom door across the room, pointing a cute little stainless steel semi-automatic at my chest.

"Well, if it isn't Ms. Martin," I said. "What a surprise. How did you get in here?"

"I convinced the pimple faced desk clerk I was Mrs. Rick Bishop here to surprise my husband. He gave me a key card. Then I hung out in the lobby until I saw you get out of the Uber."

"Aren't you the clever one?"

"I try."

"Oh, I see," I said. "You flirted with me at the bar. And you were waiting outside that alley because you knew I was in the alley. That means you must know the people who put me there."

"Mr. Weismann and I are old friends. He hired me to hedge his bets in case Bryan proved incapable of getting the package from you. Bryan was the muscle, but I'm the brains."

"So, you too are a cultural artifacts enthusiast?"

"I'm more interested in what's inside the artifact, as is Mr. Weismann."

"How much do you think it's worth?" I asked. "I'm guessing about twenty million."

Marlee chuckled. "I misjudged you, Rick. You're not as dumb as you look."

"Well, it took me longer to figure it out than it should have," I said. "Even before I finally got my hands on the necklace to examine it, I should have been asking myself why Weismann was so willing to kill over something worth less than a million dollars."

"I'd love to stay and chat, but I have someone to see," Marlee said. "Drop the box on the floor and kick it over here. And don't even think about trying for the gun on the bed. I'm very good with this and I'd not like to shoot you. I was beginning to like you until you ghosted me after I nursed you back to health."

"Yeah, sorry about that. But it's just so hard to know who you can trust these days."

"I suppose it is," Marlee said. "Now, drop the box on the floor and kick it over here, Rick."

"You can call me Mr. Bishop," I said.

"Oh? Now you're mad?"

"You don't resent it, do you?"

"Not at all. But, please, the box. I wouldn't like to shoot you, but I will."

"All right, sure," I said.

I picked up the box, threw it over my shoulder toward the balcony, and then dived out the open door for the railing. A shot rang out and shattered the glass door just as I vaulted over the railing. I hung on to the top bar for an instant, and then let go and dropped.

Frantically, I grabbed for the patio railing on the balcony below, but my left hand slipped off. I hung on with my right hand for a few seconds, but it felt like I was ripping my stitches loose, and the pain forced me to let go. I fell for another floor and grabbed the railing of the next balcony and held on that time, although the sudden stop felt like it had almost wrenched both arms from the sockets. Fighting the burning pain on my right side by trying to put most of my weight on my left, I pulled myself up and clambered over the railing. I had just rolled off the top railing onto the floor of the balcony when a bullet fired from above ricocheted off it.

I sprang to the balcony door and found it locked. So, I picked up a patio chair and used it to smash the glass. Entering the empty room, I sprinted to the door, opened it, and ran down the corridor to the stairs. Since she had wasted the time to shoot at me, I figured I had a two-floor head start on Marlee and had to beat her to the package I'd tossed off the balcony.

Trying to ignore the pain, I took the stairs two at a time and arrived on the ground floor. Then I burst out the door, jogged through the lobby to the door leading to the pool, and went out through it. I saw the package resting atop the hedges against the wall of the building. I grabbed the box and glanced both directions, but saw no sign of Marlee yet, so I sprinted for the underground parking garage.

Passing the valet stand, which was empty, I skidded to a stop. I searched the board until I found the keys to the rental and snatched them from the hook. Then I took off for the garage again. I ran down the ramp and down the aisle between the parked cars, looking left and right. Finally, I spotted the rental. I had to get out of Dodge.

A dozen feet from the car, Bryan stepped out from behind a column. He had a crutch under his right arm and held another big gun in his left pointed at me. He grinned and pulled the trigger. I never heard the bang. My head exploded in a sheet of flame. I went soaring out over a dark sea and then everything faded to black.

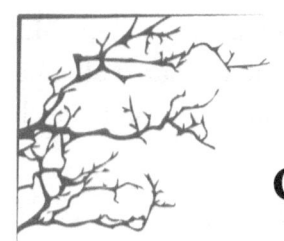

Chapter 18

A BRIGHT LIGHT WAS shining in my face and all I wanted was to sleep. I heard some irritating beeping noises and people talking who sounded far away.

"Sally," I moaned. "Sally... Sally."

"Just take it easy, Mr. Bishop. You are going to be okay."

My eyes fluttered open. A man and a woman in scrubs were bending over me.

"Where am I?" I groaned.

"You are at Sharp Coronado Hospital, Mr. Bishop, in the ER," the man said. "You've been shot, but the bullet only grazed your head. Are you having any vision problems?"

"Things were a little out of focus before, but I'm seeing okay now."

"That's fine. I'm Doctor Bennett. Are you feeling any nausea, Mr. Bishop?" He shined a light in my eyes and moved it side to side.

"No nausea. My head just hurts."

"We need to do a CT scan, but there is no skull fracture. Your pupils are normal, but we can't rule out a possible concussion. You took a serious blow to your head."

I lifted my hand to my head to make sure I still had one and felt they had wrapped my head with a bandage.

"Ouch."

"Yes, your head will feel sore for a while," Bennett said. "The bullet cut a furrow as it traveled along your skull. You were very fortunate, Mr. Bishop. It could have been much worse."

"What day is it?" I groaned.

"You can't recall?"

"I know it was Saturday when the guy shot me," I said. "I just don't know how long I was unconscious."

"Oh, all right." Bennett looked at his watch. "It's a few minutes past three on Saturday afternoon."

"Oh, good," I said. "I have a flight to catch tomorrow morning. I already missed the last one."

"Fine. Well, someone will be in to take you down for the CT scan in a few minutes. And there is a police detective who wants to speak with you once we've finished the scan."

"Terrific," I said.

"Once you're upstairs in a room, we'll give you something for the pain. I'll look in on you once you're settled in your room. We'll keep you overnight for observation. Assuming there are no complications, you may still make your flight tomorrow."

"Thanks, doc."

Bennett and the nurse left the room. I pulled out the IV needle and sat up on the edge of the gurney. The room made a few revolutions, but finally my vision cleared again. I'd had worse vertigo after a night out drinking. I stood up and found I could walk without falling down.

My sports coat was on a chair beside the door. I shrugged it on, opened the door, and peered out. There were medical people and others walking back and forth. I stepped out anyway and starting walking like I owned the place. I saw a sign with an arrow pointing toward the waiting room, so I turned around and walked the other way. The last thing I needed was Richardson wasting anymore of my time and I felt sure he was the detective waiting to talk to me.

After I finally found an exit, I left the hospital grounds.

A HALF HOUR LATER, an Uber driver dropped me off in front of Hotel Del Coronado. I went straight up to my room, packed my roll aboard, stuffed the pistol I'd found was still on the bed into my waistband and left the room.

I checked with the valet and found out someone had found my car keys in the parking garage. He brought my rental around and I bid farewell to Hotel Del Coronado. O'Donnell would probably be sore when he got the bill for the busted balcony glass door in my room after the cleaning staff discovered it.

Fifteen minutes later, I exited the 5 and stopped at the Holiday Inn Express on San Diego Avenue near the airport. I checked in on my dime and then headed to the business center to use a computer.

Bryan and probably Marlee now had the package. It was an easy guess where they had gone with it. Wherever Bryan had taken me for the first beat down. Of course, I did not know where it was. I had been unconscious going and coming. But I knew the metal building had been very close to orange groves. The scent of oranges had been overpowering. I had glanced at my watch once before Bryan had started in on me, so I had a rough idea of how long it had taken Bryan to drive me from Hotel Del Coronado to the metal farm building. It was thin, but that was all I had to go on.

First, I went to the Southern California Citrus Growers Association website and made a list of all the orange growers in the San Diego area. Then I pulled up a map and crossed off all those more than a forty-minute drive from Hotel Del Coronado. That shrunk my list to only three possibilities.

After switching the map to the satellite view, I zoomed in on each of the possibilities. Two of the sites had no buildings close to the trees I saw on the screen, but the third location had a large tan structure right in the middle of the trees and a two-story house nearby. I was sure enough that I'd found the right place to drive out to it. It was south of Chula Vista, off the 5 and on a road named Pacific Grove Road.

I got in the rental and headed back to the 5 and then drove south to Chula Vista. Ten minutes later, I took the Pacific Grove Road exit and headed east. After another ten minutes, I saw a sign for Sunbow Ranch advertising oranges, peaches, plums, and avocados. I passed the main entrance, which looked like it led to the two-story house, and then turned off the paved road onto a dirt road and drove through an open gate posted with neatly lettered "PRIVATE PROPERTY" and "NO TRESPASSING" signs.

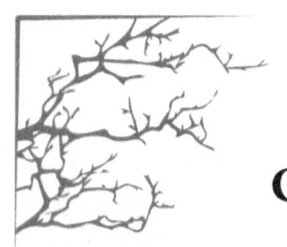

Chapter 19

CONTINUING DOWN THE road, I entered the orange grove. I stopped the car in the road flanking the orchard lanes and stared at the trees. They were lush and beautiful, their fruit-laden branches swaying slightly in the breeze. I breathed in the tangy, pungent citrus scent I remembered from my previous visit. I was certain I'd found the right place and could see the large metal building through the trees in the distance, and tried to work out how I could get to it.

Suddenly a shotgun blast stripped bare a branch of a tree right in front of the car. Shocked, I turned my head. Out the rear window of the car, I saw a man on horseback galloping toward me. His straw hat blew off his head, but he still had the butt of the shotgun pressed against his shoulder. With my avenue of retreat to the paved road denied me, I gunned the car and took off down one of the orchard lanes between the trees.

The dirt track was rough, and I bounced around behind the wheel. As I neared the end of the track, two men on foot, one with a rifle, appeared in front of me, blocking the way. I yanked the steering wheel hard left, slewing the rental into an intersecting track, sending up dust plumes behind the car and knocking a branch off a tree. The hide-and-seek chase with the shotgun-wielding horseman and the two men on foot continued across the grove until I became disoriented and had lost all sense of direction.

As I gunned the car to veer into a turn, another shotgun blast shredded a front tire of the rental and ruptured the radiator. A steam cloud enveloped the windshield, blinding me and the front of the car smashed into a tree trunk, shaking loose a barrage of heavy fruit that rained down on the car.

Finding the door jammed from the collision, I struggled out the window through the tree branches, but someone grabbed me and yanked me out. He was a thin, wiry guy, and strong and as we tussled, someone began hitting me across the shoulders and back with something that I realized was a crutch. Between the two of them, they pounded me to the ground in a few moments, and the guy with the crutch kept wailing away on me with it.

Pulling up his horse in a cloud of dust, the guy with the shotgun shouted.

"All right. Enough. Quit it. Search him and see if he's armed."

The beating stopped and the wiry guy pulled me off the ground and threw me against the back of the rental. I felt his hands going over my clothes and then snatching the pistol out of my waistband. Breathing heavily, I felt pretty banged up and half out on my feet.

"Hey, that's mine," someone behind me shouted.

I turned to look and saw it was the guy with the crutch, and realized it was Bryan. Then I remembered he had a crutch when he had shot me back at the hotel parking garage.

Bryan poked me in the back with the crutch. "Hey, I shot you," he said in astonishment, realizing who I was. "You were dead."

"Sorry I couldn't stay dead, Bryan," I said. "But I'll tell you what. You touch me with that crutch again, and you will need a pair of them."

The wiry guy shoved me. "Why don't you pick on someone not crippled, tough guy?" he said.

"I said cut that out," the horseman said, menacing the wiry guy with the muzzle of the shotgun. "Who are you?" he asked me.

"Name's Bishop," Bryan said. "He's the private detective. Let's just kill him and be done with it."

"No, not until we see what Mr. Weismann says," the man on the horse said. "It's a problem that he found his way back here. He might have told someone."

"I'm with Bryan," the wiry guy said, raising the pistol he had taken from me.

I kicked him squarely in the crotch, kneed him in the jaw when he doubled over, and then punching downward, put him on the ground with a straight right. Then I kicked the gun away just as Bryan slammed the crutch down on the back of my head. I dropped to my knees, fell over on my side, and then I curled up in a ball and went to sleep.

WHEN I CAME TO, I FOUND myself lying on the concrete floor of the large metal building I'd visited before with my wrists handcuffed behind my back. There wasn't a single part of my body that didn't hurt, especially my head. I tried to go back to sleep, but my moaning kept me awake. I heard a vehicle drive up outside and after the engine shut off, the side door opened. Andrew Weismann walked in. He pulled up the chair Bryan had tied me to, sat, and looked down at me.

"Bryan told me he had killed you inside the parking garage at your hotel, Mr. Bishop. It appears Bryan was mistaken."

"Yeah, to paraphrase Twain, the report of my death was grossly exaggerated."

"Had you been wise, you would have returned to Honolulu while I still believed the report factual. Bryan is usually much more reliable."

"Well, I don't think you should be too hard on Bryan. It wasn't entirely his fault. In fairness, he was shooting with his non-dominant hand. And you know, head wounds always look worse than they really are."

"Nevertheless, we will have to get the job right this time," Weismann said. "Marlee tells me you know far too much now."

"In fairness, you should give me a cut and let me go," I said. "After all, if it weren't for me, you would have never found the package. And I can keep my mouth shut."

"Actually, you're wrong about all that. We had already learned about Albert Brooks' brother. Why do you think Bryan showed up at his hardware store? It was only luck you arrived there ahead of him. And by turning down my bribe a few days ago, you revealed yourself a man of integrity. You wouldn't keep your mouth shut. If I let you live, you would feel duty bound to go to the authorities with what you know."

"Well, you could hire me," I said. "A private investigator is like a doctor or an attorney. When you confide in him, what you tell him is privileged."

"Don't insult my intelligence, Mr. Bishop. The authorities can compel a private investigator to reveal anything in court. Not to mention, most of them would spill their guts for a one hundred-dollar bill."

"So much for my integrity, I guess."

"I no longer have any use for you," Weismann said. "But I'm curious. How did you figure there was more to the artifact than met the eye?"

"Let's trade, Mr. Weismann. I'll answer your question if you will answer one of mine."

"Surely you realize you're in no position to bargain, Mr. Bishop."

"I'm relying on your sense of fundamental fairness, Mr. Weismann. And you've already told me you intend to kill me. So what's the harm in granting a last request? Dead men tell no tales."

Weismann stroked his chin. "You make a compelling argument and I am curious, so we have a deal. You first, Mr. Bishop."

I rolled up to sit on my butt and nodded. "I was born and grew up in Hawaii and understand Hawaiian culture. When I opened the package to check the lei niho palaoa, I found an extra whale tooth pendant in the box. I knew that wasn't right. The ancient Hawaiians were very superstitious people. If the pendant somehow came off a lei niho palaoa and got lost, they would have taken it for a bad omen and would have burned the necklace. They wouldn't have simply put a spare pendant on it. Then I compared the pendants and noticed the hairline indentation that encircled the top of the one on the necklace. I twisted it, and viola, it unscrewed and the blood red diamond fell out."

"Bravo, Mr. Bishop. You are a very observant man. Unfortunately, cleverness has earned you a death sentence. But thank you for the explanation. I'll be sure we find a way to camouflage the hairline indentation before taking the relic through customs. And I'm a man of my word. Ask your question."

"I want to know if O'Donnell has been a part of your scheme all along. I have a feeling he suckered me into something I didn't understand when he sent me here to collect the necklace."

"Ah. Yes, I can answer that question. The short answer is no. Laurence only wanted the relic. A former associate of mine in Hawaii convinced him I was out to steal it from him. He sent you here out of an abundance of caution. That wasn't part of the plan. This associate was supposed to switch the pendants and take possession of the gemstone when the necklace arrived in Honolulu. But he tried to double-cross me by encouraging Laurence to send you here to collect it. I expect his plan was to take the gemstone and then place the blame on you once you arrived back in Honolulu with it."

"So, you said former associate. I assume he's dead?"

"Not yet, but he soon will be. I've been too preoccupied with getting the necklace to worry about him until now."

"Who is the associate?"

"No one you would know, I'm sure. Let's just say that Laurence O'Donnell's daughter Kathryn has fallen in with disreputable company."

"I know a little about red diamonds," I said. "Someone I know back in Honolulu owns one. A much smaller one-carat stone. My acquaintance told me most red diamonds are one-carat or less and go for about a million per carat. The one concealed in the pendant must be around five-carats and most unusual. Any stolen diamond, especially a unique one, would be very difficult to sell these days for a fraction of its worth. What's the point in stealing one?"

"One can easily find very wealthy individuals in Asia and the Middle East who would pay close to the value of such a gemstone simply for the pride of owning something so unique and they can easily afford it. While it is neither here nor there, and none of your business, rest assured, I already have such a buyer."

"Then I suppose you're in for a big payday, Mr. Weismann."

"Indeed," Weismann said, hoisting his substantial weight from the chair. "Well, I believe I've gone above and beyond in keeping my part of our agreement, Mr. Bishop."

"Yeah, I can't complain."

"Bryan tells me he observed you speaking with a police detective on more than one occasion. So, I can't be certain what you may have told the good detective. If the authorities were to arrive here before our departure, it wouldn't look too good for them to find your dead body on the premises. So, enjoy your evening, Mr. Bishop. Bryan will be around in the morning to attend you, properly this time, before we depart."

With that, Weismann waddled to the side door and went out. I heard him lock the door and then start the vehicle and drive away.

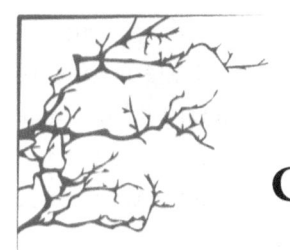

Chapter 20

AFTER WEISMANN LEFT, I got up and began searching the floor of the building. I soon found something I thought might work, a bent, brass-colored heavy duty staple, the type used with a carton closing stapler for the cardboard boxes used to ship fruit. Sitting down on the floor, I picked up the staple. Using the thumb and index finger of both hands, I straightened one end of the staple as best I could. I then pushed the straightened end into the housing of the handcuff on my left wrist and released the pawl that engaged the teeth of the single strand.

After flipping the strand off my left wrist, I brought my hands to the front and repeated the process to remove the handcuff from my right wrist. No one but the cops ever bothered to double lock handcuffs. I figured most civilians didn't even notice the tiny slot next to the keyhole or know you could insert the point at the top of a handcuff key into the slot to double lock handcuffs. I got up and stuffed the handcuffs into my pocket.

With my hands free, I walked to the side door and found it locked, as I expected. Then I went to the large overhead doors at the end. I pushed a button on a box on the wall beside the doors, but someone had cut the power to the door opener. I tried to open both doors manually, but found them locked down from the outside. The windowless building, which I assumed they used to store the picked and packed for fruit for transport, was empty except for the single metal folding chair. There was nothing for me to do but wait until Bryan showed up the following morning. I carried the chair to the wall beside the door and sat down.

SUNDAY MORNING CAME. They hadn't taken my watch, and I had just checked it when I heard a vehicle drive up outside at just past six o'clock. The engine shut off, and I heard two vehicle doors open and close. Several minutes went by before I heard someone unlocking the side door. I had already stood up, folded the chair, and held it in my outstretched arms above my head, waiting to greet Bryan. I had hoped all night that he would come alone, but I had distinctly heard two vehicle doors close. Still, I intended to go down swinging.

The door opened. The building interior was dark, and the sun wasn't yet up. I saw the dim outline of a man enter the building with a pistol in his hand. When he took his second step inside, I took careful aim and slammed the metal chair down on the back of his head and neck. He went down like an express elevator and dropped the pistol, which skittered across the floor. I raised the chair to hit him again, but in the dim light coming through the open door, I saw he was out cold. So, I dropped the chair and snatched the pistol off the floor, a large frame revolver. Peaking around the door frame, I saw a pickup truck parked outside, but I saw no in or around it.

I returned to the unconscious man, and it surprised me to see it wasn't Bryan I had waylaid. It was the rangy, wiry guy from the orange grove I had fought with. I grabbed him under the arms and dragged him to the wall of the building. Then I removed his shirt and handcuffed him to a horizontal steel support beam just above the floor that the sheets of metal siding attached to. I ripped a strip of cloth from his shirt, balled it up and stuffed it into his mouth. Then I tore off a longer strip and tied it around his head as a gag to prevent him from spitting out the wad of cloth in his mouth. His head was bleeding, so I ripped off another strip and bandaged his head.

Cautiously, I crept outside with the pistol at the ready. Seeing no one, I closed the side door and locked it with the key the guy had left in the lock. Then I approached the pickup truck. It surprised me to find a second man lying on the ground on his back, in a pool of blood soaking into the hard-packed dirt. Someone had cut his throat and when I knelt beside him I saw it was the guy who had ridden the horse during the pursuit through the orchards. I couldn't figure out why, but it seemed clear the rangy guy had killed his partner before entering the building to kill me.

Checking the pickup truck, I found the keys in the ignition with the key to the handcuffs on the ring. I got in, cranked the engine, and backed up. Then I followed the gravel road toward the two-story house in the distance. It was getting lighter out, so I left the headlights off.

I stopped the truck and killed the engine just before I left the tree line and would enter the open. Unless they had already left, I expected Weismann, Bryan, and probably Marlee Martin were inside the house, so I couldn't risk driving right up to it.

Getting out, I stayed in the trees and made my way to a point where I could approach the house directly from the back. Then I sprinted across the open ground.

There was a screen door opening onto a screened-in back porch and through it I saw a backdoor to the house beyond. Mounting the steps, I opened the screen door slowly and slipped quietly across the porch to the back door. I turned the knob on the backdoor and found it unlocked. I opened it inward and slipped inside.

Hearing voices from somewhere at the front of the house, I walked quickly up a hallway and then stepped through an open door into a bedroom after making sure it was empty. Standing just inside the open door, I listened. I could still hear the conversation and could make out it was two men and a woman talking, but I couldn't make out the words.

I could have escaped easily enough. But I was determined not to leave without the package. Stepping out into the hallway, I crept toward the voices. The tone changed, and it sounded like the people were arguing, but I still couldn't make out the words they said. I only hoped to surprise them, and maybe the argument would serve as a distraction. I expected Bryan and Marlee both had weapons but I hadn't seen Weismann with a gun.

I inched closer and closer, and could make out some words now, but didn't have enough context to understand what they were arguing about. I came to a dining room and knew the three people were just beyond it in the living room. Suddenly, three gunshots exploded. I dropped to a knee where I was with the revolver raised, thinking they had discovered me. But I saw no one enter the dining room from the far end. Then I heard the front door open and slam shut. I hurried through the dining room and burst into the living room, scanning right and left with the pistol.

Bryan lay on his back on the floor with a bullet hole in his forehead and Weismann sat slumped sideways in a chair with blood on the chest of his shirt. A semi-automatic lay on the floor beside Bryan. I kicked it away as I sprinted to the front door. Opening it, I peeked out and saw Marlee walking toward Bryan's gray sedan with the package tucked under her left arm and holding the silver semi-automatic in her right hand down at her side. I stepped out onto the porch and leveled the revolver in a two-handed grip.

"Stop and put down the weapon!" I shouted.

Marlee stopped immediately.

"Rick?" she said, her tone betraying her surprise. "I wondered what was keeping Mike. I was just on my way to check. But I guess you saved me the trouble."

"Were you going to kill him, too?" I asked.

"What can I say, Rick? I don't like to share. And twenty million is twenty million."

"Put the weapon down, Marlee," I said. "Like you once said to me, I wouldn't like to shoot you, but I will."

Marlee's shoulders slumped. Then the package was falling as she spun toward me, raising the little silver gun. I shot her twice in the chest as her shot struck a post on the porch three feet away from me. The pistol dropped from her right hand and she collapsed onto the ground.

I walked down the steps and out to her. After kicking the pistol away, I knelt beside her. I put my arm around her shoulders and lifted her slightly. She looked up at me.

"Looks like nobody gets anything," she said.

"I'll get my bonus to go with all the beatings," I said. "I guess I came out on top this time."

Marlee smiled up at me. "Sorry I won't make it to Hawaii," she said. Then her head sank back, and she stopped talking because she had stopped living.

I lowered her to the ground gently and used my fingers to close her eyes. Then I stood up and looked down at her.

"Probably for the best. I would have had a hard time explaining you to my girlfriend."

Then I picked up the box from the ground and walked back into the house.

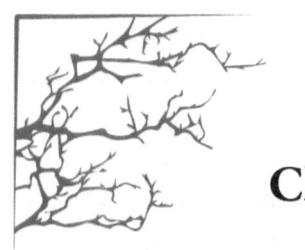

Chapter 21

BACK INSIDE THE LIVING room, I checked Weismann for signs of life but found none. I didn't bother with Bryan. I'd never known of anyone surviving a gunshot to the center of the forehead. Then I opened the box to check the lei niho palaoa. I unscrewed the replacement pendant and found the red diamond still inside.

My first inclination was to take a vehicle parked outside and drive back to my hotel to clean up and then on to the airport. The problem with calling and waiting for the cops to show up was they would probably insist on keeping the lei niho palaoa as evidence. But knowing they would probably find my fingerprints, they might take my leaving for Honolulu as evidence I was guilty of something. I didn't want to risk getting extradited back to California on some bogus charge. Talking to the cops was my best chance of convincing them I was innocent and had only killed Marlee in self-defense. I took out my phone and called Detective Richardson in Coronado.

After giving Richardson a summary of the situation, he told me he would head to the ranch and would call the San Diego County Sheriff's Department because the crime scene was in their jurisdiction. Richardson was still interested because he hoped to find the murder weapon used to kill Albert Brooks, the homicide he still had to solve. I told

Richardson not to bother sending an ambulance, since everyone at the scene was long past needing medical care. Then I hung up.

About forty minutes later, four uniformed San Diego County deputies arrived and secured the scene. I told them about the dead body up the hill amidst the orange groves in front of the metal building and the guy I'd left handcuffed inside the building. Two deputies stayed with me at the house and the other two headed up to the metal building.

Fifteen minutes later, Richardson showed up with two county homicide detectives, a crime scene crew, and a county coroner's investigator. I led the detectives through the events that had occurred step by step, beginning with the pursuit through the orange groves when Weismann's men had taken me prisoner after causing me to crash my rental car.

"You mean to tell us all these people died over an old necklace made of hair?" asked the county detective named Adams. He seemed incredulous.

"Not exactly," I said. "Let me show you something."

I led them over to the table where I'd left the lei niho palaoa and unscrewed the pendant. Then I tipped it up and the red diamond dropped into my hand. I showed it around.

"What kind of jewel is it?" Richardson asked.

"It's a red diamond," I said. "Very rare and very valuable, and a red diamond this size is unusual. Most of them in existence are one-carat or less. This one is probably at least five-carats and probably worth around twenty million dollars."

"Where did it come from?" Detective Adams asked.

"I don't know," I said. "But since Weismann was trying to smuggle it inside this necklace, you can probably bet it's stolen."

"I know a guy with the FBI that investigates stolen jewelry crimes," Adams said. "Let me see that, and I'll call him."

Adams took the diamond and walked out into the hallway to make the call.

Cruz, the other county detective, looked at me. "So, you killed the woman in the front yard?"

"She gave me no choice," I said. "I'd just entered the back of the house after escaping from the farm building up the hill when I heard the three shots that killed these guys. I went out the front door and tried to stop her. But she shot at me and I had to shoot back."

Detective Adams walked back into the room. "The FBI thinks this diamond was probably part of the haul from a jewelry heist that happened two years ago in London. They are sending two of their agents from the San Diego field office here with a photograph and the details to examine it."

"Well, that's one mystery solved," I said.

The two uniformed deputies that had gone up the hill to the farm building came in with the lanky guy I'd left handcuffed inside the building. He still had handcuffs on his wrists.

"He admitted to killing a guy we found outside the building," one deputy told the county detectives.

"What's your name?" Cruz asked the prisoner.

"Rudy Jimenez," the wiry guy said. "I work here."

"Who is the dead guy up the hill, and why did you kill him?"

"His name is Bill Franklin. He was the foreman here. I just wasn't thinking straight. Marlee told me we had to kill Bill and the others and then we could sell the diamond and go away together."

"Marlee?" Cruz said. "The blonde? Were you two involved?"

"Yes, she's my girlfriend."

"You mean was your girlfriend," Cruz said. "She's dead."

"What? Dead?"

"Don't take it too hard, Jimenez," I said. "She was on her way up the hill to kill you when I shot her."

"Take him to the station and book him for murder," Adams told the two deputies. They escorted Jimenez from the room.

"It's going to take the rest of the day to clean up this mess," Cruz said. "We've got four dead bodies."

"I think I've given you all the help I can, detectives," I said. "And I've got a flight to catch in about two hours."

"I guess you will miss it," Adams said. "Once we finish here, we need you to come to the station for more questioning."

"There is nothing else I can tell you," I said. "Jimenez already confessed and everyone else is dead."

"He's right, guys," Richardson said in my defense. He had surprised me.

"Let's cut him a break for cooperating and let him make his flight," Richardson continued. "We'll all be better off when he is out of San Diego and back in Honolulu. You can always call him if you have more questions."

"How about it?" I asked Cruz and Adams. "That all right with you?"

"Yeah, okay, you can go," Adams said. "Just leave a number where we can reach you."

I gave him my phone number, and he wrote it in his notebook.

"My rental is wrecked out in the orange groves," I said to Richardson. "Any chance you could give me a ride to my hotel?"

"Do I look like a taxi service, Bishop?" Richardson asked.

"You would do yourself a favor giving me the ride, Richardson," I said. "On the way, I can help you wrap up your Coronado murder and your chief will think you're a swell homicide investigator."

"Well, okay," Richardson said grudgingly. "I guess I'm not needed here."

I put the lid back on the box and picked up the lei niho palaoa.

"Hey, where do you think you're going with that?" Cruz said. "That thing is evidence."

"Evidence of what?" I said. "You've got the diamond. That's the evidence for all the killings."

"Yeah, but they used it to smuggle the diamond," Adams said, pointing at the box under my arm.

"So what?" I asked. "Who do you plan to charge with smuggling? Everyone is dead."

"Oh, let him take it," Richardson said. "He's right and if letting him have it gets him out of San Diego faster, believe me, it's worth it."

"Well, okay," Adams said. He turned to one of the crime scene photographers. "You guys get photographs of the hair necklace?" The photographer confirmed they had already photographed the box and its contents. "All right, Bishop, you can take it."

"Thanks," I said. I turned to Richardson. "Shall we, Detective?"

"Yeah, let's get out of here," Richardson said.

We walked out of the house and got in Richardson's unmarked car, and we drove away from the house.

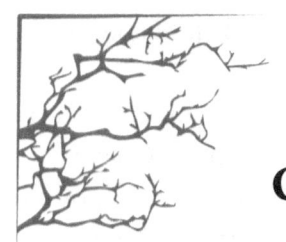

Chapter 22

ON THE DRIVE BACK UP the 5 to my hotel, I filled in the missing pieces for Richardson on the Albert Brooks murder.

"Weismann told me Bryan shot Brooks sometime after Brooks arrived at the airport with the package on a flight from New York City and before he showed up at my hotel room. Bryan was trying to get the package from Brooks for Weismann."

"But Brooks had already left the package with his brother before he got to Hotel Del Coronado?" Richardson asked.

"That's right. I took Bryan's gun, the murder weapon, from Stanley Brooks' hardware store for safekeeping after Bryan fled the scene. But he took it back from me when they captured me in the orange groves. So, the handgun on the living room floor in the house is your murder weapon."

"Well, I guess you're right about one thing, Bishop. Me solving our murder case so quickly will impress the chief."

"How do you keep your job, Richardson?" I asked. "With only a murder occurring in your town once in a blue moon?"

"I mostly investigate robberies and thefts, the usual tourist town crimes," Richardson said. "I got the murder case because I'm the senior detective."

"Well, too bad I can't hang around for a while," I said. "With my nose for dead bodies, I could help make you a full-time homicide detective. You would probably make lieutenant in no time."

"No thanks, Bishop. I'll be happy when you are back in Honolulu finding corpses for your pal, Lieutenant Chang."

"Guess you're right, Richardson. We should think of old friends first, and I'm sure David Chang is missing me terribly."

"I still can't believe it, Bishop. You've been in San Diego for less than a full week and there were five murders, one attempted murder, and one justifiable homicide. How do you do it?"

"Two attempted murders, Richardson," I said. "Not to brag, but you forgot Bryan tried to kill Stanley Brooks and me. How do I do it? As I told you, it's a gift. Sometimes life can be murder."

"Well, I'm just glad you will soon be back in Honolulu with your gift, Bishop."

Richardson pulled in to the Holiday Inn Express and stopped in front under the awning. I got out.

"See you around, Richardson."

"I hope not," he said. "Have a pleasant flight, Bishop." Then he sped away.

I went inside and took the elevator up to my room. After a quick shower, I put on my last clean shirt and put the new suit back on, although it no longer looked new at all. Then I put the box with the lei niho palaoa into my roll-aboard and called an Uber to take me to the airport.

The Uber driver dropped me at the car rental center so I could settle up. The clerk seemed understanding about the wrecked rental and I was glad I had rented the car on my client's dime and had paid extra for the damage waiver. I left the rental car counter and took the free shuttle to the departures terminal.

Ninety minutes later, I boarded the American flight to Honolulu. My ordeal in San Diego was over and I hoped I wouldn't be coming back to the mainland anytime soon. Still, I had work left to do when I go home before I could stamp another successful case closed.

THE PLANE TOUCHED DOWN five and a half hours later at Honolulu's Daniel K. Inouye International Airport on a clear, sunny, Sunday afternoon. The weather was much like it had been the day I had departed for San Diego. With the three-hour time difference, it was 1:38 p.m. Honolulu time when I grabbed a taxi in front of the terminal. The driver took me straight to 888 Kapiolani Boulevard, Sally Jayne Fisher's condo. I needed some tender loving care after my taxing week in San Diego.

I got out of the taxi, took the elevator up, and rang the doorbell.

Cooper opened the door. "Yes? Oh, my goodness. Mr. Bishop?"

"In the flesh, Cooper. Just a little mangled."

"Miss Fisher told me you were flying back today. Did anyone die in the crash?"

"The plane didn't crash. Just the usual work-related complications, Cooper. Is Miss Fisher in?"

"Oh, yes. She's in the lounge. Come in, sir. Come in."

"Thank you, Cooper."

"Shall I get you some steak for that face, sir?"

"No, that's okay. Run along and make me a drink with a little backbone in it, Cooper."

"Yes, sir. Right away."

I headed for the lounge to tell Sally her sweet and bloody was home again.

"Hello, baby," I said.

Sally gasped. "Ricky, is that you?"

"That's a good question. But if it's not me, what are you doing with a strange man in the house? You know how jealous I am."

"Stop wisecracking and come through so I can have a look at you."

"Yes, ma'am."

I sat down on the sofa beside her, and Sally examined my face.

"Oh, my poor baby," she said. "Come here. Look at your little face. Tell me what happened, Ricky."

"Oh, it's a sordid little tale, full of heroic deeds. You wouldn't be interested."

"Well, suit yourself."

"It would take too long to tell, and besides, you know how modest I am."

"All right."

"I'd feel like I was bragging."

"Forget it then."

"Well, the whole thing started six days ago..."

"You don't have to tell me if you don't want to," Sally interrupted.

Cooper came in with a cocktail on a tray.

"Here you are, sir. Your drink."

"Thank you, Cooper."

"Will that be all?" he asked, glancing from me to Sally.

"Yes, Cooper," Sally said. "Thank you."

Sally held my face in her hands and continued assessing the damage.

"I think this is the worst beating you've had since I met you. You have bruises on top of bruises."

"Don't let the bruises fool you, honey. I'm still the same old pretty face beneath them. And to be fair, it was multiple beatings. Hey, remind me to show you my stab wound later."

Sally let me go and shook her head. "Well, I hope you finished that awful case."

"Only the mainland part of it," I said. "I've still got a few loose ends to tie up here at home."

"Oh, Ricky, please take a few days off and heal a little before you go back to work. I don't think you would be safe out on the streets."

"Why wouldn't I be safe?"

"Someone might think you're dead and bury you."

I laughed. "You're so mean."

"You were gone for almost a week," Sally said. "I'm sure you must have met some girl in San Diego. You probably met a full harem."

"Only one, sweetheart. An attractive blonde with curves in all the right places."

"Ricky!"

"Don't be jealous, darling. We only had drinks together. Besides, she's dead now."

"That's terrible."

"How about a little music?" I asked, getting up and moving to the piano.

"No, I'm mad," Sally said, crossing her arms and pushing out her bottom lip.

I sat down on the piano bench. "You know you're the only girl for me, sweetheart. What would you like to hear?"

"Nothing. I'm mad."

I played and sang an old Frankie Valli tune I knew Sally liked.

"You're just too good to be true

Can't take my eyes off of you

You'd be like heaven to touch

I want to hold you so much

At long last, love has arrived

And I thank God I'm alive

You're just too good to be true

Can't take my eyes off of you."

I continued serenading Sally, and the ice had thawed by the time Cooper announced that dinner was served. We sat down to dinner and I looked forward to getting that tender loving care later at bedtime.

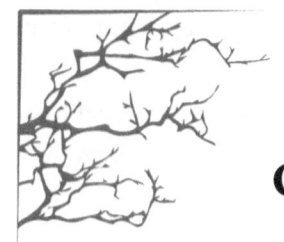

Chapter 23

FIRST THING ON MONDAY morning, I went down to the Bishop Museum to see an old friend, Paul Kealoha, a conservator-restorer. Paul was a professional responsible for the preservation of artistic and cultural artifacts at the museum of natural and cultural history. I took along the lei niho palaoa and the spare pendant.

I walked back to Paul's office and knocked on the frame of the open doorway. Paul, seated behind his desk, looked up and grinned.

"Rick, it's been a minute," he said. "Come on in."

"Hello, Paul. You have time to look at something for me?"

"Sure, Rick. What have you got?"

"I removed the top from the box and put it on the desk in front of Paul."

"Oh, my. This is a well-preserved lei niho palaoa. Where did you get it?" Paul's brow furrowed. "Wait a minute, Rick. This wouldn't be the Kalani'opu'u lei niho palaoa that I've heard that Laurence O'Donnell is donating to the museum, would it?"

"The one and the same," I said.

"What are you doing with it?"

"O'Donnell sent me to the mainland to courier it back. Guess he doesn't trust the post office."

"Well, it is quite valuable, not to mention an important Hawaiian cultural artifact."

"True enough, Paul. But there is a slight problem with the lei niho palaoa."

"What's the problem?"

"Watch this."

I unscrewed the hollow pendant and separated it. Ever seen a whale tooth pendant like this, Paul.

"No way," Paul said. "The pendant might be authentic, but someone altered it with modern tools. It is shameful someone would do such a thing."

I reached into my pocket and took out the extra pendant.

"I think they also substituted that pendant for this one, which I'm willing to bet is the original."

Paul took the pendant and inspected it. "You are correct, Rick. See this mark? It is inscribed on every authentic Kalani'opu'u artifact I've ever seen. As you can see, this pendant on the necklace doesn't have the mark."

"Well, since you agree and are the professional, I was wondering if you could switch them back. I wasn't about to try it myself because I didn't want to risk damaging the lei niho palaoa."

"Sure, no problem. You have time to wait? It should take me no more than a half hour."

"Yes, I've got plenty of time."

While Paul worked on the ceremonial necklace, I filled him in on the story behind it and how someone had used it to smuggle a stolen gemstone into the country.

"I can't believe Mr. O'Donnell would be involved in such a thing," Paul said. "The board here holds him in the highest esteem as a defender of science and culture."

"I have no reason to believe he was involved in the smuggling scheme," I said. "But someone may have manipulated him."

Despite my blathering on, Paul completed the switch in a little less than thirty minutes and left no evidence he had altered the necklace. I took the hollow pendant from him and put it into my pocket.

"What now, Rick. Are you leaving the Kalani'opu'u artifact with us?"

"No can do, Paul. O'Donnell paid eight hundred thousand dollars to repatriate the necklace, and deserves the privilege of handing it over to the museum acquisitions committee himself. Now that you've restored it, I'll deliver it to him as I agreed to do."

"I understand, Rick. I'm just glad you noticed someone had switched the pendants and preserved the original."

I thanked Paul for his valuable assistance and left the museum. Then I got in the car and drove to my office.

I PARKED THE MUSTANG in the alley to avoid another confrontation with Mrs. Wong, my landlady. Then I walked around front, unlocked the street level door and went up the stairs to my second-floor walkup office. I sat down at my desk, picked up the phone, and called Laurence O'Donnell. He must have been sitting with his hand on the phone because he answered immediately.

"Mr. Bishop, I expected you yesterday. You better have a good reason for not delivering the lei niho palaoa to me yesterday, as agreed."

"Yeah, I apologize, Mr. O'Donnell, but after the trial and tribulations in San Diego, after landing at the airport, I had to go to the hospital for an emergency blood transfusion."

"Whatever, Mr. Bishop. Your shenanigans have not impressed me in the least. Now where is the lei niho palaoa?"

"Don't worry, Mr. O'Donnell. I have it here with me and it's safe and sound."

"Fine. I'll cancel my 11:00 o'clock meeting and drive to your office immediately to pick up my property."

"No, don't do that," I said. "I've got an emergency appointment with my dentist and I was just leaving. I have a few loose teeth from getting knocked around in San Diego trying to get your precious package back for you."

"When the devil can I expect you to complete the assignment I gave you, Mr. Bishop? I've tired of all the delays. I should have my head examined for hiring you in the first place."

"Careful, Mr. O'Donnell. You'll give yourself an aneurysm or something if you don't calm down. I'll tell you what. Give me your address and I'll drop off the package at your place around eight o'clock this evening."

"Oh, very well. I live at eight nineteen Kahala Avenue. Do you know where it is?"

"Of course," I said. "That's close to the Kahala Hotel and Waialae Country Club."

"Fine, I shall expect you at eight o'clock sharp. Do not be late, Mr. Bishop." O'Donnell slammed the phone down.

The chances of me getting a five star Yelp review from O'Donnell seemed slimmer than ever, but there was a method to my madness. I wanted to go to O'Donnell's house for a chance to meet Andrew Weismann's Honolulu connection, his former associate who had tried to double-cross him and steal the red diamond out from under Weismann.

I had no reason to believe the person would be at O'Donnell's that evening. Weismann hadn't even given me the name. He had only described the person as the "disreputable company" O'Donnell's daughter Kathryn had fallen in with. I at least hoped to speak with her and find out the identity of Weismann's former associate.

It seemed my client was well off since he lived in Kahala, one of Oahu's most elite neighborhoods, where some of the wealthiest people on the island lived. Besides the locals who lived there, Kahala real estate served as vacation housing for mainland celebrities and business moguls, which is why some considered the neighborhood the "Beverly Hills" of Hawaii.

Of course, I had exaggerated my ailing health. I was feeling pretty good, all things considered. But I was a little tired after the previous night spent with Sally and wanted a nap. Sally was the most wonderful girl in the world. Just like the song I'd sung for her, too good to be true. She was rich and drop dead gorgeous. Sally had only a single bad flaw. She wanted to get married. But no one was perfect. I hung the do not disturb sign on the outside office door knob, locked the door, and stretched out on my sofa. I was soon fast asleep.

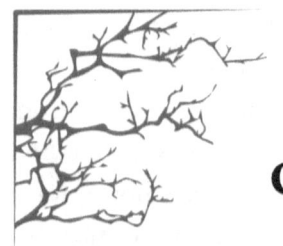

Chapter 24

I WOKE UP AROUND THREE in the afternoon feeling refreshed. I felt like I was up for another round of Sally's physical therapy that evening after I finished work. After unlocking the door and removing the do not disturb sign, I sat down at my desk. I didn't want to discourage walk in traffic because I would need another case as soon as I wrapped up the one I was working on. Rolling my shoulders to work out a few kinks, I picked up the phone and called my good friend David Chang down at the Honolulu Police Department on South Beretania Street.

"Homicide, Sergeant Rowden speaking."

"Who taught you how?" I asked.

"Taught me how to do what?"

"Speak."

"Oh, is that you, Bishop?"

"No, it's Santa Claus. I'm calling to inform you that you're officially on the naughty list."

"Why don't you buy yourself a new joke book, Bishop? You're not funny."

"Everyone's a critic," I said. "Let me talk to Lieutenant Chang."

"Hang on."

After the transfer went through, David came on the line.

"Lieutenant Chang."

"Hello, David. It's me, Rick."

"I thought you were in San Diego. Some detective from there called for a reference."

"I was, but I'm back now."

"Well, hang on a minute, Richard. Let me get the Alka-Seltzer."

David came back on the line after a few minutes.

"Okay, I can stand it now. Who is dead?"

"I hate to disappoint you, David, but I'm not calling about a corpse. I just got back in town and it will be a few days before I can start finding dead bodies for you."

"In that case, how was the mainland?"

"Tiring."

"You know, Richard, even though I worked every day you were away, last week felt like I was on vacation."

"Thanks, I appreciate that, David. I'm always happy to hear I've made someone's life just a little brighter."

"So, if you're not calling about a murder, why are you calling?"

"To give you a heads up. I may need you and Sergeant Rowden later this evening."

"What for?"

"I'm trying to shut down a trans-Pacific jewelry smuggling ring. I took care of the mainland end, and I'm hoping to identify the Honolulu connection this evening."

"What the devil are you talking about, Richard? Did you get hit on the head again?"

I told David all about my experiences in San Diego and how I was after an unidentified local conspirator involved in the attempt to smuggle a valuable stolen gemstone into Honolulu.

"What does that have to do with me unless the guy gets murdered?"

"If I run into him at Laurence O'Donnell's house this evening, he might try to get rough," I said. "He won't be happy when he finds out the package he's expecting doesn't have the red diamond inside it."

"All right, Richard. Call my cell phone if you need backup. Just don't kill anyone. There hasn't been a murder in Honolulu since you left for San Diego."

"Thanks, David. I'll do my best. But keep your phone handy."

I hung up the phone. Even though he hadn't said it in so many words, I could tell David was happy I was finally back. That's just the way it was with us guys. We had a hard time to expressing our true feelings to each other without feeling weird about it.

WHILE BISHOP PONDERED his thoughts about why men were less likely to talk about their feelings to other men, another scene played out across town in the wealthy district of Kahala. A red Cadillac XT5 pulled into the driveway of a stunning beachfront trophy estate on Kahala Avenue. The private and gated residential estate compound featured two separate building wings seamlessly connected by an entry courtyard, lush tropical landscaping, an oceanfront great lawn, and a gorgeous multi-purpose pool. A curvaceous young blonde stepped from the car. Her brother, with a drink in his hand, met her at the front door.

"Well, good afternoon, my dear sister," he said in a sarcastic tone, his speech slurred by one too many cocktails. "You're looking simply ravishing."

"How would you know how I look, Jeremy?" the woman replied, not hiding her annoyance. "You're blind drunk, as usual."

"Oh, drop dead, Kathryn."

"You miserable excuse for a man. Why don't you sober up for five minutes and look at yourself in a mirror?"

"I did once, so forget it. By the way, our dear father would like to have a word with you in the library."

"Tell him to go to..."

"I already did. Now it's your turn."

"I don't care to. Now get out of my way, Jeremy."

"Suit yourself, but Tommy Takahashi is in there with him."

"Tommy?"

"Uh-hum. Is that your heart I hear going pitter-patter?"

"Oh, shut up."

"They are in there arguing. You better get in there and protect your lover, darling."

Kathryn strode to the library and went in.

"I'm not interested in your opinion, Mr. Takahashi," Laurence O'Donnell said bluntly. "You've helped quite enough. I took your advice about sending the private detective to San Diego after the lei niho palaoa. The man has been an unmitigated disaster."

"Laurence, that is why you should call him back right now. Tell him you're sending me to pick up the lei niho palaoa for you at his office instead of waiting for him to bring it here this evening."

"No, I've made the arrangements. He will deliver the lei niho palaoa here at eight o'clock."

"Oh, hello Kat."

"Hello, Tommy."

"There you are, Kathryn. Mr. Takahashi and I were just discussing delivery of the lei niho palaoa. The detective he advised me to hire is bringing it here this evening."

"Yes, I heard the argument all the way from the front door," Kathryn said cooly. "I'm surprised you've put up with him this long, Tommy. He is like arguing with a tree stump. Come on, let's leave my dear stepfather to simmer down."

"I want to talk to you, Kathryn," O'Donnell insisted.

"Well, I don't want to talk to you. Come along, Tommy."

"Try to talk sense into him, Kat," Takahashi said. "I've told him I heard Andrew Weismann already has men in town to steal the lei niho palaoa. It's foolish waiting until eight this evening for the private detective to bring it here. He may not even have it by then."

"At least let Tommy deliver it to the museum for you in the morning, you stubborn old goat," Kathryn said to O'Donnell.

"I'll do no such thing," O'Donnell replied testily. "The museum's board of directors is hosting a luncheon in my honor at the club tomorrow afternoon. I will present them with the lei niho palaoa there in person. That's what I wanted to speak to you about. I want you and your half-witted brother to attend the luncheon. And I'm counting on you to keep him sober."

"Jeremy is not my responsibility," Kathryn said. "And while I can't speak for him, I'm not attending your stupid luncheon. Is that all?"

"No, that is not all. You listen to me, Kathryn. When you got into your trouble with the police, dear stepdaughter, the court released you on probation under my supervision. If I should report to the authorities that you have violated the terms of your probation, you will most certainly go to jail."

O'Donnell produced a small, square plastic bag containing white powder.

"Did you really believe I was unaware you're still taking drugs? I found this in your bedroom this morning."

"You dirty snoop! You have no right going into my room! What's the matter? Aren't you satisfied with living off the fees you siphon from mother's estate?"

O'Donnell stepped toward his stepdaughter with a raised hand. "How dare you! You insufferable..."

Takahashi intervened by stepping between them and putting a hand on O'Donnell's chest to arrest his advance. "That's enough, Laurence."

"Well, just shout and threaten all you want to," Kathryn said with a hostile glare. "After my twenty-first birthday on Friday, you better start looking for another source of income. My probation ends and I will receive my inheritance from mother's estate."

"You know very well it's not about the money for me. But I'm sure your boyfriend here would certainly like to get his hands on it."

"Look you, I don't care if you are an old man," Takahashi protested. "I will not stand here and listen to your insults."

"Tommy, please," Kathryn said.

"No, baby, I won't take it. I'll knock him on his pompous backside."

"Go on, Takahashi. Go on. It would give me great pleasure to call the police and have you locked up."

"When I finish with you, you won't be calling anyone."

"Tommy, no. Can't you see that's what he wants?"

"Oh, all right," Takahashi said. "Come on, Kat. Let's get some fresh air."

"I want to say one more thing," Kathryn said. "Just remember, Father. My probation expires on Friday. After that, I'll be out of this house and out from under your supervision. Until then, stay out of my room and keep your filthy paws out of my underwear drawer, you old pervert."

O'Donnell waved the tiny white powder filled plastic bag. "And if I should report you to your probation officer first thing in the morning?"

"I wouldn't. If you do that, you will not only stop controlling any part of my inheritance, you will stop breathing."

"Get out!" O'Donnell roared. "Both of you. Get out!"

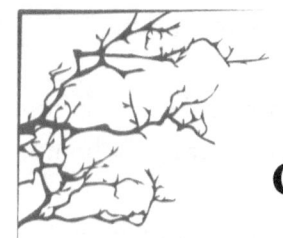

Chapter 25

A LITTLE BEFORE FIVE in the afternoon, I locked up the office and took O'Donnell's package down to the car. After locking the box in the trunk, I drove over to Sally's condo.

When I rang the doorbell, Sally answered the door.

"Hi, Ricky."

"Hi baby. Where's Cooper?"

"I gave him the night off. I thought after your week away on the mainland, we would have some alone time after our date tonight."

"Sorry, honey, I've got to work tonight."

"No, Rick. Can't you put whatever it is off until morning? You can't break another date tonight."

"Come on, Sally baby. A job is a job and I'm going to collect that big fat bonus this evening."

"And a date is a date. I won't let you break this one. Please, Rick. You promised you wouldn't break another one."

"Darling, O'Donnell already thinks I've been stalling him, and I have to deliver the package tonight."

"Look, I want to hire you to protect me this evening. I've been receiving mysterious phone calls, and I'm in fear of my life."

"Really?"

"You've got to take the job. Old friends come first."

"Well, I've got to shower before I can start working."

"You mean you will take it?"

"After ten this evening, baby. Just as soon as I get back from delivering the package to O'Donnell and collecting the bonus."

"Rick! You... you date breaker."

"I'll tell you what. I'm sure you're tired from working all day and you gave Cooper the night off. We've got time. I don't have to be at O'Donnell's place until eight. I'll take you out for a nice early dinner first."

"What?"

"Yeah, a nice meal will do you good, honey. Now I've got to shower and change clothes."

"Oh, you..."

AT SIX, SALLY AND I were at the Maoni on Waikiki, dancing to the live music while we waited for our food order.

"Rick?"

"Uh-hm?"

"Talk to me. You haven't said a word since we got here."

"Oh, I'm sorry, baby. I just have a lot on my mind. Honey, you're the best dancer on the floor."

"That's no compliment. We're the only couple dancing."

"Details, details."

"I know you brought me here only as a peace offering for breaking our date tonight."

"Honey, whatever made you think such a thing?"

"We'll this is a far cry from the place you took for dinner two weeks ago."

"Oh, I don't know. What's wrong with Kaleo's shrimp truck? No crowds. Peaceful. Beautiful beach views."

"No cover charge."

"Well..."

"And the entertainment. A server who wiggled her bum for you and the AM radio playing mostly static."

"Young lady, you just have no appreciation for the arts."

"You can't mean the server's wiggling bum?"

"Well, no, and that's a good topic to let this conversation die on. Our server is putting our food on the table."

We left the dance floor and sat down at our table.

"Oh, Rick, can't you put off delivering that package until tomorrow morning? It would be heaven. Just you and me together for one entire evening. No one to..."

"Ricky!" shouted a woman from across the restaurant.

"Oh, no," Sally said.

"My sentiments exactly," I replied when I recognized the woman approaching our table.

It was an old girlfriend of mine, Koko Mahelona. Koko and I had dated for a couple of years. She worked for my best friend, Joe Rose, as the bar manager at the Likelike Club. We broke up after her best friend seduced me and we accidentally slept together.

Koko was the kind of girl who makes even the tongues of your shoes hang out. Any other time, I would have enjoyed seeing her again, since it seemed we were back on speaking terms. But with Sally sitting beside me, I felt like a condemned man having his last meal while they were preparing the lethal injection.

"Rick Bishop, of all people," Koko said. "Don't you look as handsome as ever? It's been a long time. I never see you at the club anymore."

"Uh... yes, it has been a long time. A long, long time. You hear that, Sally?"

"Oh, I did, Rick. I did."

"Koko, this is Sally Fisher. Sally, Koko Mahelona."

"Ms. Mahelona, I can't tell you how happy I am to meet you," Sally said. "Rick has told me so little about you."

"Oh, that's sweet. Ricky, I was just thinking the other day about that week we spent together in Bora Bora. Oh, that was fun. Rick, how could you ever forget an experience like that?"

"Don't worry, dear," Sally said sweetly. "I'll see that he never does."

Ouch, I thought.

"Wonderful," Koko said, flashing me a toothy smile. "My boyfriend is around here somewhere. You two simply have to join us at our table. For old times sake, Rick?"

"Well, I, ah..."

"Oh, by all means, Rick," Sally said icily. "Catching up on old times sounds like fun."

"Oh, just look at the time," I said, pointing at my watch. "Another time, Koko? We just stopped in for a quick bite. I have to work tonight and I really better get going."

"Oh, Ricky," Koko pouted. "Well, okay."

"Can you grab a cab, honey?" I asked Sally.

"What?"

"You need a few bucks for the cab? Oh, no. On second thought, you only live what, about twenty-four blocks away? The walk will do you good."

I leaned over and kissed Sally on the forehead.

"Bye, baby," I said. Then, I turned to Koko. "Good seeing you again, Koko. We'll have to do it again soon." Then I hot-footed it out of the restaurant.

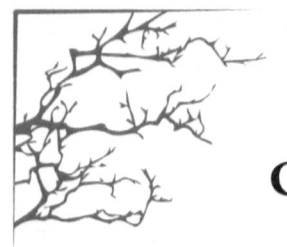

Chapter 26

I DROVE OUT TO KAHALA. And at eight o'clock sharp, I was ringing the doorbell at the O'Donnell mansion with the package under my arm. It was a big house, all right. A beachfront with two separate wings connected by an entry courtyard featuring a lot of tropical landscaping. A tall, blond young man opened the door.

"You must be the detective. My name is Jeremy."

His breath reeked of booze and he had slurred his words.

"Blow your booze some other direction," I said. "Your breath would wither a lung."

"I'll have you know that my alcoholic exhalations are composed of the finest ingredients. You must have a weak stomach."

"Look, if you could just stagger out of the way, I'd like to see Mr. O'Donnell."

"Dead or alive?"

"What?"

"Don't mind me. I was only thinking out loud. Well, go right ahead. And after you've talked with my stepfather, you can find me in the bar. You will probably need a good stiff drink or two by then."

"Where can I find your stepfather?"

"Probably in the library counting my money."

I left Jeremy leaning against the front door, struggling to stay upright. I wandered down a long corridor furnished with enough antiques to make the Smithsonian blush in shame. It took me two or three minutes before I spotted the tall double mahogany doors that looked like they might lead to a library. As I approached the doors, I heard heated voices shouting beyond them. I paused for a few moments until the shouting stopped and then, when I reached for the lever-style door handle, a shot rang out.

Pulling the semi-automatic from my shoulder holster, I pushed down the lever, shoved the door open, and scanned the interior, which appeared empty. The double French doors at the back of the room stood open.

"Mr. O'Donnell?" I shouted. "Mr. O'Donnell?"

"Here," a voice said, and then a grizzled, white-haired head appeared over the back edge of the desk.

"Mr. O'Donnell?"

"Yes, yes. Come in and shut the door."

I watched as Laurence O'Donnell stood from his crouch behind the desk.

"Someone just tried to shoot me from the garden," O'Donnell said.

"Yeah, I heard the shot," I said.

"You must be Bishop."

"That's right. Don't you think you should shut the French doors and pull the drapes before someone takes another shot?"

"Yes, splendid idea. You shut them and pull the drapes. Won't you?"

"Okay, sure. I suppose I'm still in your employ."

"Be careful. He might still be out there."

I stepped out onto the patio and glanced around. Seeing no one, I holstered my pistol.

"I don't think so," I said, pulling the doors closed. "There's no one out there that I could see." I closed the drapes.

"He just missed me," O'Donnell said. "Look, you can see where the bullet struck the wall. I ducked and hid behind the desk."

"Did you see anyone?"

"No, he must have been out there on the lawn just beyond the garden."

"That's a good twenty feet from the house. You're lucky he didn't move closer. He probably wouldn't have missed. Got any idea who it was?"

"Of course. Tommy Takahashi. I just threw him out for the second time today. He went out through those doors moments before he fired the shot."

"Tommy Takahashi? The nightclub owner?"

"Yes. You know him?"

"I used to be on the Honolulu police force. I sent him up five years ago on a gambling promotion rap."

Tommy Takahashi was a hood who owned a nightclub in Chinatown. When I knew him, he ran a high stakes poker game in a back room of the club. It was also common knowledge among the cops that he was one of the biggest cocaine distributors on Oahu, but the narcotics boys had never made a case stick against him.

"Then you know what he's like," O'Donnell said. "He's been at the house since this afternoon and we've argued incessantly."

"Argued about what?"

"The lei niho palaoa. I don't know what got into him, but he has insisted on seeing it. He even demanded that I allow him to go to your office to pick it up this afternoon rather than waiting for you to deliver it this evening. When I refused, be became livid. But I insisted we would wait until you brought it this evening and then I'd lock it in my safe until the luncheon at the club tomorrow. That's when I will donate it to the museum."

"What is your connection to Takahashi?" I asked.

"My daughter has been seeing him for the past several months. And I believe he is a bad influence on her."

"Well, she couldn't have picked a better playmate than Takahashi to get into trouble."

The study doors opened and an attractive, curvaceous young blonde burst into the room, followed by the drunk young man who had let me into the house.

"Father, we heard a shot," the woman said.

"Let's go, he's not dead," the young man said, not hiding his disappointment.

"My stepchildren, Mr. Bishop," O'Donnell said, before turning to them. "I'm quite all right. Sorry to disappoint you both."

"Does it show?" the young woman asked flippantly.

"Come on, sis," the young man said. "Let's go find the guy that fired that shot. I want to give him a few pointers."

"Where is Tommy Takahashi?" I asked the woman.

"Yes, he's the man you want," O'Donnell said. "I'm sure of it."

"Don't be absurd," she snapped. "Tommy left when my dear stepfather ordered him off the property. He had already driven away before we heard the shot. What are you? A cop?"

"Do I look like a cop?"

"You're wearing too much cologne and white socks with a suit and dress shoes. Come on, Jeremy." They both walked out, closing the door behind them.

I chuckled. "Oh, she's delightful," I said sarcastically.

"That's Kathryn. The boy is her brother, Jeremy."

"I'd hate to draw straws for them."

"I married their mother, God rest her soul, and adopted them. When she passed, the court appointed me as the conservator of her estate. Kathryn doesn't come into her inheritance until she turns twenty-one and marries. Jeremy, according to his mother's explicit instructions, doesn't get his until age thirty-five. He will probably be long dead of cirrhosis of the liver before then."

"Ah, and they don't like you handling their money. Is that it?"

"Yes, precisely. I've raised those two brats and since they've been old enough to ask for money to see a movie, they have condemned me for watching over their interests."

"You said your stepdaughter got into some trouble with the police. Tell me about it."

"I'll make it brief. I hate drawn out explanations. Kathryn got arrested in Takahashi's club when an undercover police woman caught her with cocaine in the restroom. The court could have sentenced Kathryn to a year in jail, but I hired the best criminal attorney in Honolulu to represent her and he got her off with probation. It ends on Friday when she turns twenty-one, and that's also when she becomes eligible to receive her inheritance. Half of her mother's estate. And I think she plans to marry that hoodlum, Tommy Takahashi."

"And you believe he's after her money?"

"That's right. But this morning I found drugs in her room and am considering reporting her to her probation officer tomorrow for violating the terms of her probation. And she will surely go to jail."

"Well, your stepdaughter is an adult, so I don't see how you can stop her from ruining her life if she chooses."

"Yes, but she won't marry or receive her inheritance until she completes her sentence if she goes to jail. Which might be in her self-interest. I think she lacks the maturity to handle her own finances just like her alcoholic brother."

"Well, you didn't hire me to solve your domestic problems, Mr. O'Donnell," I said. "You hired me to pick up and deliver this." I placed the box containing the ceremonial necklace on the desk. "And once you've checked the contents of the box, you can pay me the bonus you promised, plus my expenses in San Diego, and I'll be on my way." I placed a type written invoice on top of the box listing my expenses, another thousand dollars.

"Yes, let me have a look at the lei niho palaoa," O'Donnell said, opening the box. "With all the drama this evening, I almost forgot all about it."

He unfolded the tissue paper and picked up the necklace, inspecting it from every angle.

"It's magnificent," he said. "The photograph I received from the auction house in New York didn't do it justice."

"So, everything is in order?" I asked. Despite what Weismann had told me before his death, I couldn't be certain that O'Donnell had no involvement in the smuggling scheme. But he didn't seem to notice that I'd had Paul Kealoha switch the pendants, and he hadn't scrounged in the box looking for a second pendant.

"Yes, quite," O'Donnell said, setting the necklace aside and reviewing my expenses invoice.

"What's this hotel charge?" he asked. "I already paid for your lodging through last Saturday at Hotel Del Coronado."

"Yes, but Andrew Weismann and his hirelings knew I was staying there," I said. "Once I gained possession of the necklace, I had to move to another hotel for my last night in San Diego."

I wasn't about to go through the entire sordid story about what had occurred in San Diego. I had done what he had hired me to do, and that's all he needed to know.

"Oh, very well," O'Donnell said. "That makes it six thousand in total." He went to a large painting on the wall, which swung open on hinges to reveal a wall safe. After checking to make sure I couldn't see the keypad on the safe, he entered the combination, opened the safe, and took out a thick stack of cash. Returning to the desk, he counted out sixty crisp one hundred-dollar bills and handed them to me.

I had watched O'Donnell count the money, so I just slipped the thick stack of bills into my inside jacket pocket.

"It was a pleasure doing business with you, Mr. O'Donnell," I said. "Please keep me in mind should you ever need the services of a private investigator in the future."

"Actually, I think I would like to hire you to take care of another matter," O'Donnell said. He replaced the top on the box, carried it to the safe, and put it inside. After closing the safe door, he swung the painting back into place.

"What matter is that?" I asked.

"I want you to take care of the business with Kathryn and Tommy Takahashi," he said. "I don't want her seeing him anymore."

"Look, Mr. O'Donnell. Like I said, your stepdaughter is an adult and can do what she wants. Even if it's making poor decisions. I don't see how you can stop her. What do you expect me to do? Drive around with them and spoil Takahashi's aim if he tries to shoot you again?"

"I want you to go see Tommy Takahashi and to discourage him from continuing to see her. Tell him I will report her probation violation to the authorities if he doesn't cease and desist and he won't get a cent of Kathryn's money."

"Well, if I did that, I suppose that would leave you in a pretty good position," I said.

"What do you mean by that, Mr. Bishop?"

"I mean Kathryn wouldn't marry him and you would continue as conservator of the entire estate and wouldn't have to disburse half to Kathryn until she met and married someone else. That could take years."

"I can understand you thinking something like that, believe me. But as much as I sometimes detest my stepchildren, I want what is best for them for their mother's sake."

"I see. But you must know, your plan probably won't work. Once Kathryn's probation ends at the end of the week, I doubt the court would reopen the case even if you brought up her probation violation to the authorities after the fact. Your leverage is only good for a few more days."

"I'm counting on you to be persuasive, Mr. Bishop. Tommy Takahashi is a hoodlum. I doubt he has an intimate acquaintance with the provisions of the law. Just refrain from sharing with him what you just told me."

"Let me sleep on it, Mr. O'Donnell. I'll give you my answer tomorrow morning. On my way out, I'll have a look around outside to see if I can find anything that could identify Takahashi as the suspect in the shooting tonight. If I find evidence that points at him, that would take care of him and you could stop worrying about Kathryn."

"Good idea, Mr. Bishop. And call me tomorrow morning with your decision."

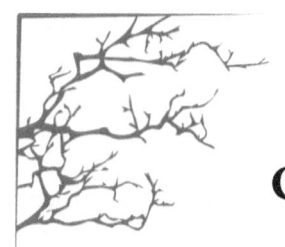

Chapter 27

I WENT OUT THROUGH the French doors and started looking around in the soft grass of the back lawn that bordered the garden. On a hunch, I stopped looking and started wandering. I was halfway past a bed of hibiscus when I spotted them. It was Kathryn and a man. In the dim lighting, I couldn't make him out. But Tommy Takahashi was my best guess. Evidently, he hadn't left the property after all.

They walked up a narrow gravel path to one of those freestanding, open-sided gazebos at the end of the gardens. I walked up close to eavesdrop on the conversation. It was Takahashi, all right.

"I don't care what you think," he said. "I didn't take a shot at the old man."

"Then who did?" Kathryn asked. "There is a detective in there now and he is going to start trouble."

"Let him. I can't worry about that now. I have to get my hands on that lei niho palaoa and switch the pendants before the old fool hands it over to the museum tomorrow. It's too bad whoever shot at him missed. Having him out of the way would have solved all our problems. Maybe it was that drunk brother of yours."

"Jeremy hates him, but he would never try to kill him. He doesn't have the guts for it."

"Well, just stop hounding me. Maybe you took the shot at him, Kat."

"Tommy!"

"Well, you have a good reason."

"I have a good reason? If what you say is true, Tommy, you have about twenty million good reasons."

"Look, I'm tired of bucking the entire O'Donnell household. Help me figure out a way to get access to that necklace for fifteen minutes so I can switch out the pendants. And if you love me, tomorrow we will find a family court judge to marry us. The old man can go to the devil."

"The marriage must wait until Friday. I won't risk deviating from the terms spelled out in mother's will. And when my stepfather goes to bed, I'll search his desk in the library. He is bound to have written the safe combination down somewhere in case he forgot it."

"I only hope you're right about the combination. But we shouldn't hold off on getting married after he threatened to notify your probation officer he found the coke in your room. He will get you tossed into the county jail. He will not give up all that money just because you're finished with your probation."

"Tommy, what's going to happen to us?"

"Oh, why don't you ask your stepfather? He's been doing your thinking for you."

"I don't have to. I'll get the safe combination tonight and we'll get married on Friday."

"Okay, but I'm leaving now and staying clear of this place until then. Call me when you find the combination and I'll come back and switch the pendants."

"But what if there is more trouble? I don't have anyone here to turn to."

"You worry it about it, baby. I've got a police record that makes yours look squeaky clean. I can't hang around here as long as that detective is prowling around. And you had better come through with that combination, or we're through."

"What? You would dump me over your precious diamond?"

"You better believe it, baby."

I would have loved to hear more, but the full moon came out from behind some clouds, and I was too close and was afraid they might spot me. So I backed away slowly and started back up to the house. I needed to warn O'Donnell in case he had written the safe combination down somewhere. If Takahashi got his hands on the necklace and found the hollow pendant that had contained the diamond missing, it might put the old man in jeopardy.

As I passed a podocarpus hedge, I noticed a funny-looking plant shoving its way out of the foliage. I was sorry I hadn't identified it sooner. It was the jumping jack garden spade variety and the person on the other end of it gave me the flat business end of the spade right over the eyes. I went down like a crapshooter making a pass.

Rolling over, I watched the moon melting and running down into my eyes. Something warm and sticky spread out over my face and turned the night red. Yeah, I was bleeding again. I guess I was showing signs of consciousness, so the person gave me a couple of sharp kicks in the ribs, and smacked me with the shovel again. Suddenly, I felt tired, so I rolled up in a bed of plumeria and went to sleep.

WHEN I FINALLY CAME around, I felt like I was swimming through an acre of mud. When you had taken as many beatings as I had, you learned to diagnose things in a hurry. The pain in my head was from getting smacked with the shove, and the pain in my side was from when they had booted me in the ribs. And the thought in my mind was something about an eye for an eye, if I still had one.

I sat up slowly and looked around. There was no one in sight and my watch said ten o'clock. I had been out for an hour. I patted my jacket and felt relieved when I found the money was still in my inside pocket. At least they hadn't robbed me.

I had made it to one knee and was feeling lonely until I saw one of the best reasons for staying home nights. Tommy Takahashi was staring up at me. And I couldn't blame him. He wasn't being impolite. Takahashi was just dead. Something on the gravel path beside him gleamed in the moonlight. I took out my handkerchief and picked it up. It was a nickel-plated 32-caliber Colt revolver and I could tell from a sniff of the barrel, recently fired. I put it into my jacket pocket and stumbled back to the house. O'Donnell opened the French doors.

"Great Scott," O'Donnell exclaimed. "What happened to you?" He wore a dumbfounded expression that looked genuine. But I couldn't be sure.

"Where were you an hour ago?" I asked.

"Here in the library. I've been in here since you left."

"I need to use the phone," I said, walking to the desk, where I picked up the receiver and dialed.

"What's going on?" O'Donnell demanded. "Who beat you up?"

"No one," I replied. "I always bleed like this on warm, humid nights."

"What?"

David Chang answered on the fourth ring, and I ignored O'Donnell's question.

"Hello, David. This is Bishop."

"Wait a minute. Just wait a minute. Let me get the Alka-Seltzer."

"What's wrong?"

"I get stomach trouble every time you call."

After several moments, David picked up the phone again. "Go ahead."

"All right, I've got a murder for you."

"I knew it. I knew it. Why can't you be a good little private detective and stop finding corpses?"

I ignored the remark. "Out at Kahala. Eight nineteen Kahala Avenue. And I think I've got the murder weapon in my pocket."

"Who's dead?"

"An old friend from when I was on the cops. Tommy Takahashi. And you better step on it. There's a drunk in the house and if he stumbles over the body, he might put it in the shower to sober it up."

"All right, Richard. I'll call Rowden and we'll be right out." David hung up.

"So Mr. Takahashi is dead?" O'Donnell asked, wide-eyed.

"You better stop sneaking up on people," I said.

"And you better stop telling me what to do in my own house, Mr. Bishop. I heard what you said about finding the murder weapon. Can I see it?"

"No. It stays in my pocket until homicide gets here."

"Whose gun is it?"

"Who said it was a gun?"

"Oh, there you are, Bishop," Jeremy said, walking into the room. "I've been looking for you. Don't you think it's about time you had that stiff drink? From the looks of you, I think you could use it."

"You seem to have sobered up since I last saw you," I said.

"Jeremy, did you have something to do with this?" O'Donnell demanded, pointing at my face.

"Hardly. Mr. Bishop has a decided advantage over me. He has muscles. I'll be in the bar."

When Jeremy left, O'Donnell turned back to me.

"Where is Kathryn?" he asked.

"I don't know. She was out in the garden with her boyfriend an hour ago and they had troubles. Then someone smacked me with a garden spade. All I know is Takahashi is lying out there in the garden with a hole in his chest that he can't explain."

"And you're sure he's dead."

"If he isn't, he is trying awfully hard to look dead. You have any guns in the house, Mr. O'Donnell?"

"You don't think..."

"No, I don't think. I just scratch around until I come up with something. What kind of gun do you own?"

"Why a 38-caliber Smith & Wesson revolver. Now you wait a minute, Bishop. Before you get any ideas about this murder, you better wait until the police get here."

"Listen O'Donnell. I've been insulted in your house, had your beautiful stepdaughter step on my ego, and got beat up in your garden. I've had a full night's work and I'm on my own time now. Where can I find Kathryn?"

"I don't know, unless she is in her room."

"Where is it?"

"End of the hall in the other wing. Fourth door on the left."

"Thanks."

"It's beginning to rain. What about Takahashi's body?"

"If you're afraid he'll catch a cold, throw a raincoat over him."

I walked out of the library, retraced my steps to the front door, and then walked down another long corridor in the other wing. I pounded on the fourth door on the left.

"Yes, who is it?"

I opened the door and went in.

"Pardon me for barging in, but someone has just beaten all the bashfulness right out of me out in the back garden."

"How dare you! You get out of my room."

"You better throw on a robe, honey. That nightie doesn't leave much to the imagination."

"What do you want?" Kathryn demanded, shrugging into a robe that she picked up off a chair. She belted it tightly around her waist.

"What did you do after Takahashi left you in the gazebo?"

"What?"

"Yes, I was there too, listening. I heard every word."

"It looks like someone shoved your face around. I think it's a definite improvement. Did Tommy catch you eavesdropping?"

"Well, if he did, he isn't gloating about it."

"What do you mean? If you've done anything to my..."

"Aren't you ready for bed a little early?" I interrupted.

"What do mean by that? I don't have to answer any of your ridiculous questions. Now if you don't turn right around and get out of my room, I'll..."

Kathryn whirled to a bureau and jerked open a drawer. But then she froze.

"What's the matter, baby? Lose something?"

"No."

I pulled the nickel-plated revolver from my coat pocket.

"Maybe this is it?"

Kathryn turned back to face me and her eyes looked like two big silver dollars when she saw the gun.

"Where did you get that gun?"

"I found it in the garden right beside your boyfriend's dead body. Now, sit down and relax."

"Tommy is dead?" Kathryn shrieked.

"As dead as the New York Time's reputation as a real newspaper," I said. "Didn't you hear anything after Tommy left you?"

"No," Kathryn blubbered. She burst into tears. "We had an argument, and I was crying," she sobbed. "I ran back to the house and came in here."

"Is there another way back to the house besides the path out to the gazebo?"

"Yes, a path that leads to the back outside doors of this wing of the house. I came right to my room. Please leave me alone."

"This is your gun, isn't it?"

"Yes, but I didn't do it. I didn't. I loved Tommy. We were getting married on Friday."

I lifted the gun and sniffed the barrel again. "Ballistics will probably show this was the murder weapon," I said. "Someone fired it recently. You better tell me everything you know."

"But I don't know anything. I didn't shoot Tommy. Someone stole my gun from my underwear drawer. Oh, please find out who did it. If the police arrest me, I'll go to prison anyway for violating my probation. Please, Mr. Bishop. Please."

Smelling the odor of burned gunpowder in the barrel of the Colt reminded me I needed to check O'Donnell's pistol. I had smelled burned gunpowder in the library when I had first arrived. But O'Donnell had told me someone shot at him through the open doors from out past the garden. That had been a lie. Someone had fired a shot inside the room, which is why I had smelled the odor of burned gunpowder.

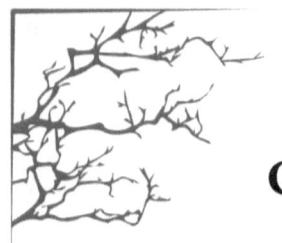

Chapter 28

BY THE TIME I GOT BACK to the library, David and Sergeant Rowden were there talking to O'Donnell.

"You see the corpse, David?" I asked.

"Yeah, the coroner and the clean up boys are on the way," David said. "Now what the devil has gone on here tonight, Richard? I can't get anything out of this guy."

I filled David in on the events of the night and then handed over the Colt. He sniffed the barrel and then stuffed it into his pocket.

"Whose gun is it?" he asked.

"Why, that's Kathryn's gun," O'Donnell said. "Where did you get it, Bishop?"

"Who is Kathryn?" David demanded.

"My stepdaughter," O'Donnell said.

"The girl I mentioned I saw talking to Takahashi at the gazebo right before someone smacked me in the face with a garden spade," I added.

"Where is she?"

"In her bedroom. I just came from there. She's upset about Takahashi."

"Better go get her, Rowden, and bring her in here for questioning," David said. "Where's her room, Richard?"

"In the other wing, fourth door on the left."

Rowden lumbered off to collect Kathryn.

"Say, Mr. O'Donnell," I said. "While we're waiting, why don't you show the nice police lieutenant your 38-caliber Smith & Wesson revolver you told me about?"

"What? Why?"

"Because I'm sure Lieutenant Chang is interested in whether anyone has fired your gun recently."

"Yes, Mr. O'Donnell," Chang said. "Let's see the gun."

"Well, all right," O'Donnell said. He went to the desk, opened the middle drawer, and took out the pistol. He brought it over, holding it like it was a dead rat, and handed it to David.

David sniffed the barrel and then handed the gun to me. I also sniffed the barrel, looked at David, and we both nodded.

"You know, Mr. O'Donnell, when I first arrived here tonight and came into the library after hearing the gunshot, I could smell burned gunpowder in the room."

"That's hardly surprising, Mr. Bishop. As I told you, someone fired a shot at me from outside."

"Yes, you told me that. But if it had happened the way you claimed, there wouldn't have been any odor of burned gunpowder in this room if someone had discharged a gun outside. You fired that shot, didn't you?"

"What? No. Of course not. That's absurd, Mr. Bishop."

"Better come clean now, Mr. O'Donnell. The lieutenant will haul you downtown and swab your hands for gunshot residue, and your story won't stand up."

"Oh, all right. Yes, I fired the gun and pretended someone had taken a shot at me. Satisfied, Mr. Bishop?"

"Why did you do that, Mr. O'Donnell?" Chang asked.

"Because I needed help to get rid of Mr. Takahashi. I didn't want my stepdaughter seeing him. I felt I had to convince Mr. Bishop he was dangerous so I could prevail upon him to help me get rid of Mr. Takahashi."

"Did you shoot Takahashi with this pistol?" David asked.

"No, certainly not. You can check. I only fired one bullet, and it's in the wall over there."

"Well, I'm still going to hold on to this for a while until we get the bullet that killed Takahashi from the coroner," David said. "After the lab makes the ballistic comparisons, as long as you've told the truth, you'll get the pistol back when we're finished with it."

"Very well, Lieutenant."

Sergeant Rowden entered the room with Kathryn. Unfortunately, she was fully dressed.

"You're Kathryn O'Donnell?" David asked.

"Kathryn Arnold," she replied. "Laurence O'Donnell is my stepfather. My brother and I kept our actual father's last name, even after the adoption."

"All right," David said. "You were in a relationship with Tommy Takahashi?"

"Yes, we had been seeing each other for almost six months."

"You were with him out in the gardens this evening, shortly before his death?"

"Yes," Kathryn said, sniffling.

I handed her my handkerchief.

"What were you and Mr. Takahashi quarreling about, Ms. Arnold?" David asked.

Between sobs, Kathryn answered. "I wouldn't characterize it as a quarrel exactly. It was only a minor disagreement."

"Didn't he threaten to end the relationship unless you accomplished something he wanted done?" David asked.

"All right. He said words to that effect. But Tommy didn't mean it. He was just upset because he and my stepfather had been arguing for most of the afternoon and evening."

"About what?"

"You would have to ask my dear stepfather," Kathryn said. "I don't know the details."

David held up the nickel-plated Colt revolver. "Is this your gun, Ms. Arnold?"

"Yes," Kathryn sobbed. "But I didn't kill Tommy."

"All right, Rowden," David said. "Read her rights to her and put the handcuffs on her."

Kathryn immediately broke into another round of uncontrollable sobs.

"Not so fast, David," I said. "I don't think she did it."

"Why is that, Richard?"

"Just a hunch, but I'm sure she's innocent."

"Well, I'm afraid the district attorney doesn't work with hunches, Richard. He insists on something called evidence to establish guilt or innocence."

"I know, David, but I'm sure I'm right about this. And if you arrest Ms. Arnold and it turns out she is innocent, as I believe she is, the arrest will be enough to violate her probation over some past trouble and she will still go to jail."

"Then she should have considered that before getting involved with a hood like Tommy Takahashi."

"Come on, David. Just give me until Friday to see if I can turn up the actual killer," I said. "You don't have to arrest Kathryn tonight."

"Now, you wait a minute, Rick. I'm very happy with what I've got, so don't you start making like Thomas Magnum."

"Oh, well, I guess you're right, David. She admits it's her gun, and being a woman scorned is certainly motive enough."

"Yeah. Rowden put the handcuffs on her."

"Right, Lieutenant."

"David, why would someone commit a murder and then leave the gun they used beside the corpse?" I asked.

"Huh?"

"I told you I found the gun right beside Takahashi's body. And later, when I talked to Kathryn in her bedroom, it took her by complete surprise when she discovered the gun was missing from her drawer. She couldn't figure out where I got it from."

"So what?"

"Do me a favor, David."

"What?"

"Give me until noon on Friday and if I don't deliver the actual killer to you, then you can arrest Kathryn then. She isn't going anywhere. Her stepfather controls all her money."

"What?"

"Is that all you can say? Just give me a few days to prove Kathryn's innocence."

"I will not. The police department can't go around letting viable murders suspects run around free just because you have a hunch they aren't guilty."

"You want to solve the murder, don't you, David?"

"I have solved it. What else do I need? I've got a suspect, the murder weapon, and a good motive."

"David, if you just killed someone, what would you do with the murder weapon?"

"Well... I'd get rid of it. Maybe throw it into the ocean."

"Well, the ocean is less than a hundred yards from the backdoor of this house. Why would Kathryn have dropped her readily identifiable pistol beside the body of her dead lover instead of running to the ocean and throwing it into the sea? You said yourself, that's what you would have done. Maybe she didn't kill him."

"Please, I didn't," Kathryn wailed. "I didn't kill him."

"You see, David?"

"Oh, you always start something like this. Maybe she left the gun beside the body to sell a story that someone stole the gun and used it to kill Takahashi. It would have looked worse for her if we had found the gun in her bedroom. Or if we had learned that she owned a gun of the same caliber used to kill him, but she couldn't produce it because she had thrown it into the ocean. I'm surprised at you, Rick. You've been up against smart killers before."

"But maybe someone did steal the pistol from her room," I said. "There are two other people living in this house who could have taken it. Mr. O'Donnell here for one. He told me earlier he went into Kathryn's bedroom just yesterday morning searching for something."

"That's preposterous, Bishop," O'Donnell said. "I didn't take the gun, and I didn't kill anyone."

"She didn't do it, David. Did you, Kathryn?"

"No, I swear, I didn't."

"Wait a minute. How do you always get me into things like this, Richard?"

"Just wait a few days, David," I said. "What can it hurt? If I can't identify the actual murderer by then, you can arrest Kathryn on Friday."

"Oh, all right, Richard. I should get my head examined for ever listening to you. But I have motive, means, and opportunity. And unless you can prove someone else killed Takahashi, I'm arresting Ms. Arnold on Friday."

"Oh, thank you, Lieutenant Chang," Kathryn said, her eyes brimming with tears. "I'd like to go back to my room now. I'm feeling a little faint. All the drama this evening has worn me out."

"I'll walk you back to your room," I said. "That all right with you, David?"

"Yes, yes. Just get out of here, Richard, and let me think for a minute in peace."

"Come along, dear," I said to Kathryn. "Let's get you into bed."

With my arm around her and Kathryn's head resting on my shoulder, we left the library and headed to the other wing of the house.

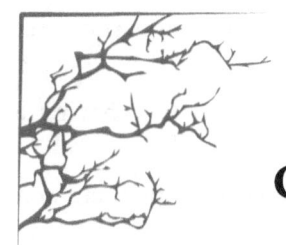

Chapter 29

I TURNED MY BACK SO that Kathryn could undress and put her little nightie back on. I helped her into bed and sat on the edge, patting her hand and speaking soothing words to her while she cried a little. She thanked me, with her eyes, for helping to keep David from arresting her.

"Do you think you can really find the actual killer before Friday, Mr. Bishop?"

"Yes, I don't expect it will be very hard," I said. "I'm pretty sure he will come to me."

"Why?"

"Because I have a good idea who killed Tommy and why," I said. "If I'm right, he will think I have something he wants badly."

"Who do you think did it?"

"Oh, you've had enough stress for one day, Kathryn," I said. "No need for you to worry your pretty little head about it."

"I don't know what I would have done without your help this evening, Rick. May I call you that?"

"Of course, dear."

"Are you married, Rick?"

"No, I've never made the trip."

"You will probably think I'm horrible for saying this," Kathryn said timidly. "But you seem like such a wonderful man. The sort of man I could imagine marrying. And after Friday, as soon as I find a man to marry, my share of mother's estate will be a little over fifteen million. I'd love having a wonderful man to share it with."

"Well, dear, I'm sure there is a perfect guy out there and you will meet him soon enough."

Kathryn sat up in bed and put her arms around me. I felt the wetness of her tears on my face as she nuzzled hers against mine.

"Please forgive me for being so forward," she whispered. "But I was thinking of you, Rick. I would make you a good wife and we would have plenty of money and never want for anything."

"Oh, that's sweet, dear," I said. "But I already have a wealthy girlfriend I really don't want to lose. And now that she has learned to talk about marriage sends me into a panic attack, she doesn't bring it up that often anymore."

Kathryn cried a little more while clinging to me. I felt bad for her, but didn't really know how to explain to her I wasn't the marrying kind.

"That doesn't mean we can't be great friends until you meet that special guy you're meant to marry," I said.

I helped her lie back down, hoping I'd made her feel just a little better.

"Will you answer a few questions for me, Kathryn?"

"Yes, if I can," she whimpered.

"I overheard you and Tommy talking about the necklace pendant and the diamond. How did he get involved in that?"

Kathryn sighed. "A man Tommy had done business with called him from the mainland."

"Andrew Weismann?"

"I think so. Tommy never mentioned his first name, but I know his last name was Weismann."

"All right, go on, dear."

"The man knew about my stepfather's obsession with historical Hawaiian artifacts. Evidently, he pressured a private collector in London to sell him a rare lei niho palaoa. He then put it up for sale through a New York auction house and told Tommy to make sure my stepfather was aware of it. The man seemed to know he would want to buy it."

I found that interesting. It was the first I'd heard that Weismann had been behind the sale of the necklace all along.

"Why did O'Donnell believe Weismann was in competition with him for the lei niho palaoa?" I asked. "It seems O'Donnell sending me to San Diego after the necklace threw a wrench into Weismann's plan to smuggle the diamond all the way into Honolulu, which is what it seemed he intended."

"That was also Tommy's doing. Weismann was going to pay Tommy one million dollars to intercept the diamond and deliver it to Weismann's buyer here in Honolulu. But somehow, Tommy figured out what the gemstone was, and that it was worth twenty million dollars."

"And he got greedy?" I asked.

"Yes, Tommy wanted all the money. He told my stepfather it would be too dangerous for him to go to San Diego himself and convinced him to hire you to go get it and to courier the necklace back here. But you took so long to accomplish it that Tommy was running out of time. He had to get access to the lei niho palaoa and switch out the pendants before stepfather handed it over to the museum."

"Do you know who the buyer was Tommy was supposed to hand off the diamond to?"

"Tommy never told me the name. All I know is it was a man from mainland China who was supposed to meet Tommy at his club tomorrow evening. And the buyer intended to slip the diamond out of Honolulu inside a diplomatic pouch so that customs couldn't interfere."

"Did Tommy tell anyone else about his plan to intercept the diamond to sell himself and keep all the money?"

Kathryn yawned widely before answering. "No. He didn't even share all the details with me. Just some of them. And I'm sure he told no one else anything."

"Could someone else here in the house have overheard Tommy telling you about the diamond and his scheme?" I asked.

Kathryn didn't answer. Exhausted, the poor thing had succumbed to sleep. I didn't wake her. I had learned enough to fill in a few more pieces of the puzzle and felt even more certain I knew who had killed Tommy Takahashi. And that person would have to move fast if he intended to get his hands on the diamond in time to deliver it to the Chinese buyer at Tommy's club the following evening.

I tucked the bed covers under Kathryn's chin, shut off the lights, and left the room. I checked the bar off the living room for her brother, Jeremy, on the way back to the library, but he wasn't there. Back in the library, I found O'Donnell alone at his desk.

"Where are the police detectives?" I asked.

"Outside with the coroner examining the body," O'Donnell said. "I was just putting the finishing touches on the speech I'm delivering at the luncheon tomorrow."

"Where is your stepson?" I asked. "He seems to be conspicuously absent."

"In the bar, I expect. That's where he spends most of his time."

"I just checked, and he isn't there."

"Then, perhaps he retired to his bedroom to sleep off his excessive libations."

"Where is his room?"

"Up the hall, third door on the right, before you get to the living room."

I bid O'Donnell good evening and headed to Jeremy's room. Finding the room empty didn't surprise me. Stifling a yawn myself, I called it a night and left the house, headed for 888 Kapiolani Boulevard. I supposed my face could use about a mile of bandages. I hoped Sally wouldn't mind.

IT WAS MIDNIGHT WHEN I rang the doorbell. Cooper answered the door wearing plaid onesie pajamas.

"Yes? Oh, my goodness. Shall I get some ice and the first aid kit, sir?"

"If it wouldn't be too much trouble, Cooper."

"Right away, sir. No trouble at all. Miss Fisher is in the study, sir."

"Thank you, Cooper."

"Hi," I said, walking into the study.

"Well, look what the cat's dragged in. It's about time. You said you would be here at ten and it's gone on midnight."

She sounded mad, but when I got closer, Sally saw my face.

"Oh, Rick, not again."

"Uh-huh."

"Your poor little face."

"Yes, my poor little face."

"Well, you just stretch out on the sofa and I'll get some ice and the first aid kit."

"Thanks, sweetie, but Cooper is already on his way."

I lay down on the couch, stretched out, and groaned.

"Feel better?"

"Yes. Got a pillow?"

Sally lifted my head and sat down on the sofa, laying my head in her lap.

"I'll hold your head up. How's this?"

"Uh-huh."

"You comfortable?"

"Yes, baby. How about you?"

"Uh-huh. This is nice. C'mere, Ricky."

Sally began kissing my lips, which was nice since my lips were the only things on my face that didn't hurt.

"Oh, honey, you're reading my mind," I said.

We didn't notice when Cooper came in.

"Here's your ice and the first aid kit, Mr. Bishop," Cooper said. Then he gasped. "Oh, my goodness!" he exclaimed.

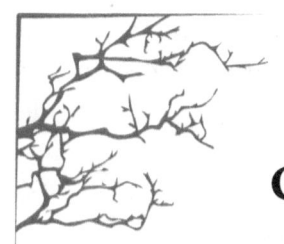

Chapter 30

THE NEXT MORNING, COOPER made pancakes, and I had breakfast with Sally before she left for Waikiki to manage her surfing and beach fashions shop.

"Ricky, if we got married you could work for father and quit the silly private detective game," she said.

"Please, honey, let's not talk about marriage. Spiraling into a panic attack just isn't what I need right now while I'm on the mend."

"That's what I'm talking about, Rick," Sally chided. "You must know you are suffering brain injuries every time someone bashes your head in. As much as it pains me to admit it, Rick, I'm nothing like your country's first lady. I simply couldn't find happiness living with a man who hadn't two spare brain cells left to rub together and who depended completely on me to keep his nappies changed."

"Don't be so dramatic, darling. It is not like I get beaten up every day. I've just had a run of bad luck."

We finished breakfast discussing more pleasant things, and Sally left for work. I took a shower, got dressed, and left for the office after Cooper applied fresh butterfly bandages to the cuts above my eyes.

After I unlocked and opened the door of my office, I scooped up the pile of bills from the floor the postal carrier had shoved through the mail slot and carried them to the waist basket for filing. I had just unfolded the paper and started on the crossword puzzle when my phone rang. I put down the pencil and picked up the phone.

"Bishop Detective Agency. If your husband is dead and you pulled the trigger. I can help, but the fee will be bigger."

"Is this Richard Bishop?" a male caller with a British accent asked.

"That's right."

"Mr. Bishop. This is Reggie Davey, calling from Nassau."

"Hello, Mr. Davey. What can I do for you?"

"It's more a question of what I can do for you, Mr. Bishop. I'm employed with Great Bahamanian Casualty Company. We insured a rather large red diamond taken in the burglary of a London diamond exchange on High Street two years ago."

"Yes?" I said, wondering why Davey was calling me.

"The American law enforcement authorities in San Diego, California, recovered the gemstone last week and returned it to my firm. It seems from the report that you played an integral role in the recovery. I've confirmed that with the authorities in San Diego."

"I see."

"My firm had offered a ten thousand dollar reward for information leading to the recovery of the diamond. If you would be kind enough to furnish me with your mailing address, I'll be happy to put a certified check in the mail to you."

"You want to send me a check for ten thousand dollars, Mr. Davey?"

"Yes, old chap. If it wouldn't be a bother."

"No bother at all," I said. I recited my mailing address quickly before I started to hyperventilate.

"Thank you, Mr. Bishop, for your kind help in the matter. You may expect the check within a few days."

"Thank you, Mr. Davey."

"Cheerio," Davey said, before hanging up.

It seemed the lessons I'd learned from my dog-eared copy of *Think and Grow Rich* were finally paying off. My ship had come in. With an extra ten thousand coming in, I could catch up on my past due car payments, give Mrs. Wong six months of advance office rent, and still have money left over to take Sally on a nice vacation.

After marveling about my good fortune for an hour, I looked at the clock on the wall. It was almost 11:00 a.m. and my expected visitor still hadn't arrived. Had my theory been wrong? Bored with the crossword puzzle, I got up and ran hot water in the sink and threw in a handful of laundry detergent. Then I stretched my clothesline along the back of the office and tackled the pile of dirty laundry I had accumulated.

As I washed the clothes in the sink, I hummed the tune of "The Sparkling Diamond" song from the musical *Moulin Rouge*. Sally and I had caught the Honolulu Community Theatre's performance of the Broadway musical at the Diamond Head Theatre the year before. Soon I was singing the words.

"A kiss on the hand may be quite continental.

But diamonds are a girl's best friend.

A kiss may be grand.

But it won't pay the rental on your humble flat.

Or help you feed your pussycat."

Between the flowing tap and my singing, I didn't hear the office door open. But I heard the male voice call out.

"Mr. Bishop?"

I stopped washing and shut off the water.

"Back here behind the socks. Careful of the clothesline. I'll be with you in a moment."

I dried my hands and stepped out from behind the hanging clothes. My expected visitor had arrived, after all.

"I thought you were a detective," Jeremy Arnold smirked. "Not a washerwoman."

"That's the rumor," I said.

"Do you always wash your laundry in the office?"

"Only on Tuesdays. What can I do for you, Jeremy?"

"I believe you have something that rightfully belongs to me," he said.

His breath had that familiar boozy odor of a whiskey barrel. But Jeremy seemed less intoxicated that he had when I'd met him at his stepfather's house.

"And that would be?" I asked.

"I think we both know," Jeremy said. "A hollow whale tooth pendant containing a valuable jewel. I already checked the lei niho palaoa. Someone already switched the pendants. I assume that someone was you."

"And if I did, what makes you think I'd give it to you, Jeremy?"

"This," he said, producing a large semi-automatic.

"My, that's a big gun you have," I said. "Where did you get it?"

"It's mine."

I supposed everyone in the O'Donnell household had their own artillery.

"If you had a gun of your own, why did you take Kathryn's gun to kill Tommy Takahashi?"

"That's absurd. I didn't shoot Takahashi. If it was her gun, I suppose my dear sister killed him. Maybe she found out he was only after her money."

"That's possible, and if it's true, I guess she was also the one who worked me over in the garden."

"That was probably Takahashi. According to stepfather, you sent him to prison once, so he probably didn't like you very much. It would have had to be someone strong. She might have kicked you and hit you with the shovel, but not hard enough to mess up your face like that."

"Yeah. Tell me something, Jeremy. If Kathryn goes to prison for murdering Takahashi, who gets her money?"

"Well, stepfather is the court-appointed conservator of the estate and would continue controlling it as long as he's alive. But I guess eventually I would inherit mother's entire estate."

"Tell me something else, Jeremy. It's obvious someone hit me in the face, but how did you know someone kicked me in the ribs?"

"What?"

"My injured ribs don't show. It just hurts. And I haven't mentioned getting kicked to anyone."

"What are you getting at, Bishop?"

"You don't look very strong, but if you were mad enough, I'll bet you could have done the damage with the shovel and kicking me when I was down is something I can imagine a guy like you doing pretty easily."

"That's absurd. Now give me the pendant you took off the necklace. I want to get going."

"You wanted to hang the Takahashi murder on Kathryn to get her share of the estate. That's why you used her gun and left it beside the body. You're a real piece of work, Jeremy. Framing your own sister for murder. Now give me that gun and I'll call the police and you can tell them the truth."

"I don't think so, Mr. Bishop," Jeremy said, waving the pistol around. "One more murder will not matter much. Now give me that pendant or I will show you how this gun works."

Slowly, I reached into my pocket and took out the hollow whale tooth pendant. I held it up.

"Is this what you're looking for?"

"Toss it over here, Bishop."

"One last question first. How did you find out about the diamond and the Chinese buyer? Takahashi wouldn't have told you squat about the scheme."

Jeremy laughed. "I can eavesdrop just as well as you, Bishop. Many an evening, I used to stand near the gazebo listening on the same spot I saw you standing on last night. Kathryn and her lover boy used to have all their heart to heart talks there away from stepfather's prying ears. That's how I found out."

"And you're just as greedy as Takahashi was."

"It isn't greed," Jeremy said bitterly. "Put yourself in my shoes, Bishop. Imagine having to wait nine more long years to get your rightful inheritance. Almost another decade of humiliating yourself by having to beg for every dime from your stingy, hateful stepfather. I simply saw an easy way to get my hands on some money to tide me over until my thirty-fifth birthday. I'm as entitled to it as a hood like Takahashi."

"I guess you're right, Jeremy," I said. "Here, take it." I tossed the whale's tooth at him and he snatched it out of the air.

Greed causes people to make mistakes, and Jeremy was no exception. He tucked the pistol under his left arm and twisted the pendant open to make sure the diamond was inside.

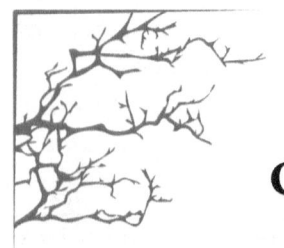

Chapter 31

BEFORE JEREMY EVEN discovered the cupboard was bare, I was already across the room on top of him. I slapped away the gun before he could get a grip on it again. Then I belted him with a right cross before putting him to sleep with a left hook. He collapsed onto the floor and the empty pendant parts skittered away across the floor.

I flipped him onto his stomach and then tied his wrists behind his back with some spare clothesline I got from a desk drawer. Then I picked up the phone and dialed the Honolulu police.

"Homicide, Sergeant Rowden speaking."

"I didn't recognize your voice at first, Rowden. You sounded almost intelligent."

"Well, well. If it isn't Richard Bishop. The private sleuth."

"Well, well. If it isn't Sergeant Rowden. The private sloth."

"Huh?"

"Look it up. S-L-O-U-T-H. The three-toed variety."

"I will."

"Before you get started, let me talk to Lieutenant Chang."

"Hang on, funny man."

"Lieutenant Chang."

"David, it's me Bishop."

"For crying out loud, Richard. Who's dead now?"

"I'm not calling about a corpse, David. Takahashi's murderer is asleep on the floor of my office. Can you come over and collect him?"

"Who is it?"

"Jeremy Arnold, O'Donnell's stepson."

"The drunk? How do you know he did it?"

"He confessed."

"You beat it out of him? The DA won't like it."

"No, I beat him after he confessed."

"Why did you do that?"

"He also slipped up and admitted he worked me over in the garden last night. You know my stance on an eye for an eye. He had it coming."

"All right, Richard. I'll get Rowden and we'll be over."

"Can you step on it, David? I have a luncheon to attend at the Waialae Country Club and it starts at one o'clock this afternoon."

"You're going over to hear O'Donnell's speech, Richard? That surprises me. I didn't think you even liked O'Donnell."

"I don't. I'm out to prove the guy wrong who said there was no such thing as a free lunch. And they really know how to put on a feed at the Waialae Country Club. Bye." I hung up the phone and looked down at Jeremy. He was still sleeping.

I had just put the phone down when it rang. I picked it up.

"Bishop Detective Agency. When you're in trouble, we come on the double."

"Oh, no. You're doing the slogans again. That one was so bad that I don't know what to say."

"You don't know what to say? Try this first. Hello, Rick."

"Oh, brother."

"Once you've mastered that part, say, this is Sally."

"Hello, Rick. This is Sally, idiot."

"Well, hello. Is this Sally Idiot the belle of Kapiolani Boulevard of the Honolulu Idiots?"

Sally laughed. "Oh, you idiot. This is Sally Fisher, the girl who dates the Bishop Detective Agency."

"Sounds like a fine agency. Are they reliable?"

"Very seldom."

"Oh?"

"I can tell you more after I find out what I'm doing tonight."

"You're going to give your houseman the night off again and the Bishop Detective Agency is going to march through your front door, single file, and show you what the true meaning of ecstasy is."

Sally chuckled. "What time is all this meant to begin?"

"How long will it take you to pucker up?"

"Um, about two seconds."

"Well, I won't arrive until seven, so don't hold it until then or you will end up looking like Kim Kardashian."

"You're terrible. But I'll give you one more chance. You better be at my place at seven o'clock."

"Or?"

"Or my place will be off limits to a certain private detective until further notice."

"Sally, I'll be at your place at seven, come high water or anything else you can think of."

"I think I might hold another man in reserve, just in case."

"It would be a waste of manpower. Wait and see. You will get more man than you can handle at seven o'clock."

"All right. We'll see."

The door opened. David and Rowden walked in.

"The cops are here, baby. I've got to go."

"Okay, Ricky. Just make sure your attorney bonds you out in time for you to get to my place at seven."

"Yes, dear. Bye."

"Bye."

I hung up.

"So, this is the guy?" David asked, looking down at the slumbering Jeremy. "You sure he isn't dead?"

"No, he isn't dead, David."

"Okay. Rowden, get him up and down to the car."

"Right, Lieutenant."

Rowden picked Jeremy up off the floor, threw him over his shoulder, and went out.

"He's a big strapping boy that Rowden," I said.

"Rick, you should lay off Rowden. He does good work. Now fill me in on what that guy told you."

I told David how Jeremy had admitted to killing Takahashi to get the red diamond for himself and how he had framed his sister to get her half of the family inheritance.

"He slipped up and mentioned someone kicking me in the ribs last night when there was no way he could have known unless he was the one who did it."

"Well, good work, Richard. I guess your new girlfriend is off the hook."

"Hush, David. The walls could have ears. And Kathryn is a cute girl who can make a man beat his chest and do the Tarzan yell when she wears a revealing nightie. But were just good friends. Sally Jayne Fisher is the only girl for me."

"Uh-huh. Just keep telling yourself that, Richard."

David picked up Jeremy's semi-automatic off the floor and left. I freshened up, put on my jacket, and then locked the office and headed for the country club luncheon.

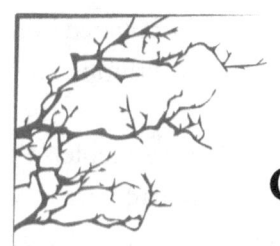

Chapter 32

I TURNED THE CAR OVER to the valet and walked inside. It wasn't often I got the chance to dine at Waialae Country Club. I bellied up to the buffet and loaded a plate with cheeses and breads from a charcuterie board, chicken salad croissant sandwiches, Thai noodle salad with shrimp, layered penne pasta bake, and broccoli salad. I spied a tray of mini strawberry shortcake cups and another of mini cheesecakes that I planned to sample later for dessert.

Just as I reached the end of the buffet line, I bumped into Kathryn Arnold. She wasn't a wearing the black silk negligee I'd last seen her in, but the form-fitting dress she had on did a good job of highlighting her feminine curves.

"Rick, how nice of you to come," she said, embracing me.

I could tell Kathryn was genuinely happy to see me by the way she kissed me. I blushed a little when I had to pull away first to avoid suffocation. It seemed she had finished mourning Tommy Takahashi.

"I'm surprised to see you here," I gasped, trying to get my wind back.

"I hadn't planned to come, but my dear stepfather promised me this morning to get me the best lawyer in Honolulu to help with my minor legal problem. He wanted me and Jeremy to both come. But when we couldn't find Jeremy, I decided to make nice and attend. It would have humiliated him if neither of us had attended. Appearances are everything to my stepfather."

Kathryn hooked her arm in mine and led me to a table. We sat down and she scooted her chair close. If she had been any closer, she would have been sitting in my lap. A server came by and gave us both a glass of bubbly.

"Well, your stepfather won't need to hire an expensive lawyer for you, my dear," I said. "You're no longer a suspect. The police have arrested Tommy's killer."

"Really?" she asked in astonishment.

"Yes, you're off the hook and can finish your probation quietly."

"Oh, Rick. You actually did it. You must be the best private detective in Honolulu."

"Only because I'm shrewd, brilliant, and loaded with talent."

Kathryn chuckled. "And so modest."

"Yes, that, along with my boyish good looks."

"So, who killed Tommy?"

"Well, you might not be as happy about that part," I said. "It was your brother, Jeremy."

Kathryn's hand flew to her mouth. "Jeremy? Are you sure?"

"I'm afraid so," I said. "He confessed. But I wouldn't feel too bad about it. He also admitted he framed you for the murder, hoping to get your half of the family inheritance."

"What! That rat. I hope they give him the chair."

"Well, Hawaii abolished the death penalty in 1957, two years before Hawaii became a state. But I'm sure Jeremy will spend many years in the penitentiary."

"I simply can't believe he killed Tommy just to get my half of mother's estate."

"He didn't. He was also angling to get the diamond and the twenty million," I said. "Jeremy confessed he learned about it by eavesdropping on your conversations with Tommy when you were in the gazebo."

"That scum. Prison is too good for him."

We chatted about other, more pleasant things while we ate our lunch. Then, the president of the museum's board of directors introduced Laurence O'Donnell, and he gave his speech about the importance of repatriating Hawaii's stolen cultural artifacts. I didn't really hear a word of it because Kathryn placed her hand on my thigh just as O'Donnell started talking and it made my imagination run away with itself.

After the speech, O'Donnell presented the King Kalani'opu'u lei niho palaoa to the museum. I golf clapped along with the other attendees. Afterward, everyone returned to the buffet table for dessert, but I gave up on having the strawberry shortcake cups and mini cheesecakes. Kathryn hadn't removed her hand from my thigh and I was feeling a little light-headed and didn't want to risk walking.

The crowd started to thin. In the lobby, I extracted myself from Kathryn's surprisingly powerful grip and said goodbye. But only after receiving another kiss. After promising to call, I staggered breathlessly out the front door to retrieve my car.

AFTER RETURNING TO the office, I took a nap on the sofa. After the big buildup, I needed to build my energy reserves so I wouldn't disappoint Sally. I woke up around six, shaved at the restroom sink, and then put my jacket back on and headed for Sally's condo. I rang the doorbell at seven o'clock sharp.

Sally opened the door and smiled.

"You actually showed up on time. I can't believe it."

"Well, believe it baby," I said, walking inside and closing the door. "I'm about to show you just how reliable the Bishop Detective Agency can be."

I followed Sally into the lounge. She mixed us a couple of tall, cool drinks and then we sat together on the sofa and kissed. I told her about the luncheon, most of it, and how I'd wrapped up the case.

"I'm so glad that the dreadful case is over and that you're safe from getting beaten up again."

"Sally, I believe you're beginning to appreciate having me around."

"Well, the piano would get awfully dusty if you weren't."

"Oh, that's sweet."

"Rick, if you haven't eaten since lunch, you must be starving. I had Cooper make us some sandwiches before he left."

"Who wants food at a time like this?" I asked. "Lights down low, a beautiful girl beside me. I'm from the old school, baby. Just give me wine, women, and song."

"Well, there's wine in the kitchen. There's a woman beside you, and you know where the piano is if you want to sing."

"Sally, you're so clever and so right."

"So, are you going to play and sing to me, Ricky?" Sally asked sweetly.

"You are a wonderful girl to sing to," I said. "But first I have just one other desire."

"Is that right?" Sally asked with a grin. "What is it you desire, Ricky? Anything I can help you with?"

"Uh-huh. I think I'd like that sandwich now."

"You dog!"

Don't miss out!

Visit the website below and you can sign up to receive emails whenever Larry Darter publishes a new book. There's no charge and no obligation.

https://books2read.com/r/B-A-HAUD-TLHAD

BOOKS 2 READ

Connecting independent readers to independent writers.

Also by Larry Darter

A Jacob Dedman Novel
The Dedman Emergence

Howard Drew Novels
Omerta
Darker Angels
LA Deadly
Laurel Canyon
The Pendulum

Malone Mystery Novels
Come What May
Fair Is Foul and Foul Is Fair
Cold Comfort
Foregone Conclusion
Foul Play
Black Deeds
Perchance To Dream

Malone Mystery Novels Box Set: Come What May, Fair Is
Foul and Foul Is Fair, Cold Comfort
Live Long Day

Rich Bishop Novels
Follow the Money
China Doll
Life Can Be Murder

Rick Bishop Novels
The Girl on the Beach
Dead End
Trouble in Paradise

T. J. O'Sullivan Series
Mare's Nest
Honolulu Blues
The Chinese Tiger Ying
Frisky Business
Missing Time

Standalone
All Our Yesterdays
Malone Mystery Novels Two Book Set No. 1

Watch for more at www.larrydarter.com.

About the Author

Larry Darter is an American author best known for his crime fiction novels written about the fictional private detective Malone. He is a former U.S. Army infantry officer, and a retired law enforcement officer. He lives with his family in Oklahoma.

Read more at https://www.larrydarter.com.

www.ingramcontent.com/pod-product-compliance
Lightning Source LLC
Chambersburg PA
CBHW021000180626
46814CB00003B/1179